the VANDALS of TREASON HOUSE

by Nancy Veglahn

Illustrations by Marilyn Miller

Xerox Family Education Services

XEROX

I

City of New Glasgow
County of New Glasgow
State of Connecticut

The Court having heard the evidence and being fully informed, now finds each of the following defendants guilty as charged of Malicious Mischief and willful damage to a house at 4214 Orchard Lane:

Marie Angela Bellotti
David Adam Keller
Arnold H. Schmidt, and
Isabelle da Silva.

Each of the said defendants is sentenced to serve one year in the State Reformatory.

It is further ordered, however, by reason of the fact that this is a first offense for each, that the sentences be suspended, subject to the following conditions:

1. Each of the above named juveniles shall submit to the Court a five-hundred-word essay entitled, "What I Have Learned About Vandalism"; and shall

2. Perform useful service in repairing damages to said house, up to one hundred hours as needed, under the supervision of the owner, Mr. Hooper Cline.

Carleton McGruder, Judge.

"What I Have Learned About Vandalism"
by Marie Angela Bellotti

To Judge McGruder and Whom It May Concern:

We decided to put these essays together so nobody would try to weasel out or put the blame on the rest of us. Since the essay bit came from Ham Schmidt's brilliant suggestion, I thought he should go first, but everybody else said I should because I talk the most. That doesn't mean I like writing 500-word essays! But since we have to do it we are going to tell you our side of the story, like Ham said.

(That's 79 words already. 87 if you count the "To Judge McGruder" part—but I guess I can't count that.)

2

It all started at the Carnival. That's the Nathaniel Hawthorne School Sixth Grade Carnival we had the last Friday of the school year. It was supposed to raise money for some playground equipment and band instruments and stuff.

Well, it was a disaster. A total flop! There we were in the gym with all those booths and paper streamers and confetti all over and balloons flying around, you know. Some of the booths were really neat, too. Our assistant principal, Mr. North, even sat on one of those diving board things over a tub of water, so you could dunk him by hitting a target with a ball. I was a gypsy fortune teller, and David Keller and Ham Schmidt worked in the cakewalk booth, and Izzy da Silva sold balloons.

Only nobody came. Maybe a couple of dozen parents and a lot of little kids who didn't have any money anyway. And then toward the end a bunch of junior high and high school kids came and said how corny everything was and dunked Mr. North six or seven times and went around popping balloons. Ham Schmidt's big brother Will was there with a lot of his friends, because Will had to give Ham and David Keller a ride home afterwards. You could see Will didn't like the idea much.

Izzy and I were supposed to take a bus home. But it took so long to clean everything up we missed it, and it would have been half an hour before the next one came, so when some of these older kids offered us a ride home we said sure.

(350 words!)

They were all mad because the Youth Recreation Hall had been closed down. Not enough money, I guess, and the City Fathers decided they could do without that. So these bigger kids said, "Let's have some fun before we go home."

I asked them to let me out. I knew my folks would be ticked off if I didn't come straight home. But they said it would just be for a few minutes and we'd have some fun. It's sort of exciting to have high school kids talk to you like a person, instead of an insect.

So we went out to this crumbling old house. You could tell absolutely nobody had been in it for years, Judge. These older kids said, "Who cares about this place, anyway? Nobody!" And you could see that nobody did.

(That's 487 words. The other three can finish this, if I don't get done in my allotted space.)

My first thought was, that it looked kind of spooky. But of course

"What I Have Learned About Vandalism"
by David A. Keller

Sir:

I'm not going to finish Marie's sentence for her, just because she's too lazy to go a few words over 500. Before I go on with the story of what happened the other night, I'd like to say a few things about vandalism.

4

In 406 A.D. an East German tribe called the Vandals ripped through Gaul and all around the Mediterranean Ocean, burning and looting. Ever since, their name has been used for acts of random destruction. Which is one way to get remembered, I guess.

My father's dictionary says vandalism is "willful destruction of the beautiful." According to my dictionary, vandalism means "willfully or maliciously defacing or destroying public or private property." It seems to me there's a lot of that going on, and it's not all by kids.

I suppose what we did was vandalism, all right. It was stupid, too. As Marie said, these older kids we were with thought the whole thing up and we just sort of followed along.

We were all mad that night. The four of us sixth graders were disgusted because we made fools of ourselves at that carnival for nothing, and the others were just as mad about the Recreation Hall being closed down. What can you do when you're mad? Yell at your little sister, maybe, or pick a fight with somebody, or smash something.

There was a lock on the front door of this old house, but it was easy to climb in a window. The shutters were all rotten and hanging from rusty hinges, and most of the glass was broken out.

I was surprised at how big the place was, when we got inside. Somehow it looked smaller from the outside. A couple of the boys had flashlights, so we looked around for awhile, just jumping out from be-

5

hind corners to make the girls scream and stuff like that.

There wasn't much of anything in there. I guess maybe a lot of other vandals had been there before us. There was a bunch of old furniture crammed onto a sort of back porch, but that was all.

At the end of this big front hall was a long stairway with a curving banister, like the kind you see in movies about fancy houses in the olden days. So of course we had to try sliding on it.

That part was really fun. Shooting around that curve in the dark, not knowing when you'd land in a heap at the bottom, and everybody laughing and yelling—it was like a Halloween party or something.

Then two or three started going down at once, and then I guess about ten kids were sliding down and the thing creaked and cracked and went over.

Honestly, we hadn't broken anything until then, and nobody meant to break that. It just happened.

But maybe we figured since we broke that banister we might as well break some more things. Some kid found a chair upstairs and tossed it down. Another guy had a can of spray paint, and he sprayed that around and wrote things on the wall with it. Come to think of it, some of those kids must have planned on tearing up that place because they also happened to have jackknives and some of that aerosol whipped cream stuff. So before long the house was pretty much of a mess.

I guess I've got more than 500 words by now, so I'll let the other two tell how we got caught and

everything. But I'd just like to say that I have learned something about vandalism. Anybody can be a Vandal, like, without thinking; even kids who never got in trouble before.

"What I Have Learned About Vandalism"
by Arnold H. Schmidt

Dear Judge:

It was my idea that we should give you our side of the story, though I didn't mean put it in writing for heaven's sake! Like I said in court, nobody ever listens to kids.

See, when you get in trouble and your parents or teacher or somebody is mad at you and you try to explain, they don't hear what you say. They just get madder and madder and finally you give up and quit trying.

Our side of the story is this:

Like Marie said, we were riding with these certain bigger kids and we had to go where they went, didn't we?

And then when we got inside we were just fooling around, it was no big deal. Until we saw that stairway. That's another thing you probably wouldn't understand. It was like the banister was *telling* us to slide down. I could almost hear it whispering "Come on, come on." Sounds stupid, but it's the truth.

We four didn't do much even after the banister broke. Marie had some confetti left from that zero

8

carnival we had at school, and so we threw some of that around. I guess it got stuck in the whipped cream and paint some places. And there was some loose wallpaper sort of hanging in shreds. We pulled some of that off and wadded it up and threw it at each other. Believe it or not, that's all we did.

Then Miss Snoopy Bellotti had to go upstairs and look around, and of course Izzy followed her. So Marie yelled downstairs, "Hey, come look what I found," and Dave and I had to go up and look. It was only an old cardboard box full of dolls and junk. If we hadn't been up there when the old man came around with the cops, we wouldn't have got caught.

I heard the kids yelling "Look out!" and running downstairs, and when I looked out one of those broken windows everybody else was outside and climbing into the cars. They peeled out just before two cop cars came charging up the other way.

Those other kids shall remain Nameless, as they say, because they'd wipe us out if we told on them. But it was them that thought up the whole thing and took us there and snuck out and left us to take the blame!

So if you ask me, a vandal is just the guy that gets caught.

P.S. I see I'm short 69 words, so I'll explain why everybody calls me "Ham." My middle initial is H., and it stands for something too Horrible to mention. So somewhere back about third grade kids started calling me Ham for the H. and my favorite food. I like it better than Arnold or "Weirdo," which is

what my brother Will calls me if he isn't calling me
something worse. (And that's one more word than
I needed.)

"What I Have Learned About Vandalism"
by Isabelle da Silva

To Your Honor:

Not much is left for me to tell. The policemen
found us in the house, and when they shined their
spotlights around it looked bad for us. The place was
a mess, all right.

There was an old man with them, Mr. Hooper
Cline. You know, Your Honor, that he owns the
house and lives next door in a smaller place. I was
very much frightened when I saw him in that hallway downstairs as he was angry and shouting:
"Look! Look what they did! Animals! Animals!"

The police were surprised to find only the four of
us eleven-year-old kids. They wanted to know who
else had been there, because they didn't believe we
did all that damage by ourselves. We couldn't tell the
names of the other kids. I didn't even know most of
them. And if we told on the ones we did know, we'd
have been in bad trouble with them, too.

It was the first time I was ever in a police station.
Marie and the boys acted like they were in a TV
show or something, at first. But I think they were
scared too. They didn't say much when their parents
came down to get them. Mr. Schmidt, Arnold's

father, sort of took over then, asking why the police were picking on us and getting mad like he did at our hearing, last week.

The policemen who took me home that night were real nice.

I'm sorry my father couldn't come to the hearing, Judge. He has two jobs and he couldn't get off work. My mother had to stay home with my little brothers and sisters. But I guess she talked to you that morning while I took care of them.

At the police station and in your court room I learned some things about vandalism. I didn't know that the city has to spend thousands of dollars to fix all the broken windows every year. I know kids who write on walls and such, but I never thought about the people who have to clean up and pay for the damage.

So I know what we did was wrong.

If you count my words and it isn't 500, David Keller said I could use some of his which were too many. I can't think of any more to say.

2

Marie Bellotti tied her favorite Indian headband around her straight, black hair.

"Are you ready, Marie?" Her mother's voice sounded sort of weak and trembly, as it had ever since that night at the police station.

"Coming!" Marie swooped the covers over her bed and ran downstairs, trying not to think about how late she usually slept on Saturday mornings.

"I packed a lunch for you." Mrs. Bellotti handed her daughter a brown paper sack. "Are you sure you don't want me to drive you to—that place?" There was the quaver again.

"No, Mother! I told you we're taking bikes. It's

not so far, and we aren't sure when we'll get done. This way we can just come on home whenever . . ."

"You will come straight home, won't you? And try to do a good job, dear."

" 'Bye." Marie hurried out and kicked up her bike-stand, hard.

At least it was a nice day. She rode to da Silva's house, which was exactly like the Bellottis', only three doors down. The warm June sun felt good on her back, and the narrow strip of sickly grass by the street was turning green at last. Isabelle was waiting by her door, her curly brown hair tied up in a red headscarf.

"Off to the chain gang," Marie said grimly as they pedaled toward the south side of town. "The second Saturday of vacation, and we have to spend it grubbing around in that old wreck! Come on, Izzy, we're supposed to be there by nine o'clock."

"I can't go any faster." Isabelle's soft voice came faintly from half a block back, and Marie slowed, remembering that her friend's bike had already been used by two older da Silva children and was practically falling apart.

They rode side by side, after the traffic thinned out a bit, watching for the sign that indicated the beginning of Orchard Lane.

"A hundred hours," Marie grumbled. "That's practically a lifetime! The whole summer will be ruined."

Isabelle chewed her lip and looked straight ahead. "It's better than going to that reform school."

"Pooh, they wouldn't send us there just for playing around in a deserted house." Marie was not as sure as she sounded. She remembered the way she'd felt when the judge pronounced their sentence, like someone had hit her in the stomach.

At the Orchard Lane corner they met David and Ham, coming from their apartment house near the center of New Glasgow.

"So, the gang's all here," Ham said. "Shall we go rob a bank, fellow criminals?"

"Shut up," David growled.

They rode the rest of the way without talking.

Marie had known Isabelle da Silva all her life. She'd been in classes with the boys but had never been particularly friendly with either of them. David, who usually got the best grades in his room, seemed stuck-up and hard to get along with. Ham Schmidt was known as a show-off. He was always getting sent to the principal's office for something. It would be a terrific summer, Marie thought, spending one day a week with this bunch of losers. The hours they'd spent together preparing their essays for Judge McGruder had been bad enough.

Even Izzy was not one of her favorite friends, in spite of the fact that they lived so close and their families were always getting together. Oh, Izzy was nice enough, but she was such a mouse. It was really strange that she'd been picked up by the police, when she was so timid she'd hardly go across the street without asking somebody's permission.

"Well, there it is," David said suddenly as they

14

rounded a curve. Marie looked past the auto salvage yard on the left side of the road and saw the house, alone and neglected in its grove of trees. They parked their bikes just off the street and stood looking at it.

It seemed different in the daylight. The yard was all weeds, and a tumble-down wooden fence leaned every which way around it. The house itself was a dirty, silver color, the windows tightly shuttered except for two upstairs and one downstairs—the one they'd climbed through that night a month ago.

"So that's the precious historic building we ruined," Ham said. "Just a creepy old pile of firewood."

"Maybe it's haunted," Marie suggested hopefully.

"It's haunted, all right," said David. "By that Mr. Cline who was yelling at us that night."

"Shhh," Isabelle warned. They heard slow, uneven footsteps, and then the old man came around the side of the house. He stood there for a moment, not saying anything.

Hooper Cline looked oddly like his house. His left eyelid drooped almost shut, like the shuttered windows on the left side of the upper story. The right eye was open and very black, like the broken-out right windows. And his whole face seemed to sag. Even his skin was gray, as gray as the boards across the front and sides of the house.

"You'd better understand something right now," he said in a deep, rusty voice. "The judge put you on probation only on the condition you work out the

damage you did to my house. You agreed to come out here every Saturday until I'm satisfied, or until you've worked a hundred hours each. Don't expect me to let you off easy. If you don't show up or don't do the work, I'll see you're sent to reform school."

He meant it. Marie felt puny and helpless, looking at him and listening to his hard words. It was not a nice feeling.

"You can start by sweeping and mopping up all the floors," Cline went on. "I've put brooms and buckets and things in the hall. In a few hours I'll come back and see what you've done. The door is un-locked."

They watched him go back around the corner of the house, limping slightly. Ham kicked at a pebble.

His thin face was red and angry. "Who does he think he is?" he muttered.

"Simon Legree," said Marie. "We're nothing but *slaves* this summer. Our family was going to the mountains for two weeks when my Dad has his vacation—now I won't even get to go."

"That's nothing. I had a chance for a paper route this summer, but Saturday was the only day I had to collect," David said.

"I'm going to have to quit my baseball team." Ham spoke slowly, as though he'd just thought of that.

Even Izzy had a complaint: "The lady next door offered me a babysitting job. Every Saturday, of course."

"Come on," Marie said, "we might as well get started. Maybe if we do really great, I mean get the

17

place absolutely spotless, he'll let us off in a couple of weeks. Say, what's that?"

She was looking at a faded board on one side of the old-fashioned door. You could just make out the head of a man, only it was bald and was divided up into many little sections like a map. There was something written on each section. Marie peered at it and read:

"Caution. Hope. Spirit. Friendship. Meow."

"Meow?" Isabelle asked, looking over her shoulder.

"That's 'Mirth,' dummy," David said. "You know, laughing, ho-ho-ho. Meow! You think that's a picture of a cat?"

"All right, if you're so smart, Keller, what kind of a sign is this anyway?" Marie turned on him angrily.

"Look down here." David pointed to some writing at the bottom of the board. "It says, 'Reginald Galusha, Phrenologist.' I wonder what a phrenologist is."

"You mean you don't know?" Marie asked with heavy sarcasm.

"What's the difference?" Ham Schmidt already had the front door open. The others followed him into the wide, gloomy hallway. David tripped over the uneven floor and bent down to rub his stubbed toe. Like the others, he'd worn his oldest sneakers and grubbiest clothes. The injured toe poked through a ragged place in his shoe, unprotected.

"Ugh," Marie moaned, "we'll never get through in here."

A bare lightbulb hung down from the ceiling on twisted, black wires. Izzy tried the switch by the door, but nothing happened. "I guess nobody would pay light bills for this place," she said.

The hall floor was completely covered with dirt, broken boards, bits of plaster, paper wads, rusting cans and all sorts of debris. Wallpaper hung in ragged shreds. At the far end of the hall was the stairway, its banister lying broken beside it like a pile of Tinkertoys.

Mr. Cline had left four brooms and dust pans, two mops, two large pails of water, some rags and a huge cardboard box marked "waste."

"I'm not spending any hundred hours trying to clean up this wreck," Ham said.

"You have to," Isabelle told him in her quiet way. "We all have to. We have to pay for what we did."

"But we didn't do all this!" Ham protested. "You know we didn't. There must have been hundreds of other kids in here in the last few years. Why should we clean it up just because we were the ones who got caught? My brother says it doesn't matter what happens to an old place like this, anyway, because it's just sitting here taking up space."

"Your brother got us into this," Marie reminded him. "He doesn't seem to mind letting us take the blame. Come on, let's get started. Why don't you guys go upstairs with a couple of brooms—maybe it's not so bad up there. Izzy and I'll get to work down here and you can help us when the upstairs is clean."

It took all morning just to sweep out the front hall. Marie kept at it steadily, choking in the clouds of dust that every stroke of her broom raised, while Izzy held the dustpan and dumped load after load of stuff into the "waste" box. They could hear the boys talking upstairs from time to time. Once Ham came slinking down the stairs with a mop over his head saying in a shrill, high voice: "Oh, Sir Percy, have you come to take me to the ball?"

"Quit goofing off and get up here," David yelled, and Ham dragged back up as slowly as possible.

"He's going to let the three of us do all the work," Marie said, pausing to lean on her broom.

"Arnold's pretty mad today," Isabelle suggested. "He'll probably get over it."

"You're the only person I know who calls him Arnold."

"It's his name."

Marie shrugged and looked around. "You know, this must have been some house when it was first built. I wonder how old it is."

"Maybe a hundred years?"

"I bet it's even older than that. Look how worn those steps are." Each wooden step on the stairway dipped in the middle, the boards worn smooth by thousands of feet. For a moment Marie found herself wondering about the people who had gone up and down those stairs. When had they lived? What sort of clothes had they worn? Sometimes they had probably run lightly, happily, over the steps, and other times their feet must have dragged with trouble or sickness or old age. Whoever they were, she decided they had nothing to do with her life now, with this miserable summer.

"You could put the first floor of our house in this hall," she said. "Shall we start mopping?"

"Maybe we'd better look in the other rooms, first," Isabelle suggested. "It'd be easier to do all the mopping at once."

There were four large, square rooms on the first floor, two on each side of the central hallway. The girls' spirits drooped even lower as they looked through them, for again the floors were heavily littered and filthy.

"I never went in any of these rooms, except when we came in through the window," Marie said. "Maybe he won't make us do them."

Isabelle shook her head. "Some of those other kids were running all through the house. Look, there's confetti from the carnival."

"Oh, I gave a bag to Lu Sullivan. She and her boyfriend must've dumped it in here. Well, get your dustpan."

At noon they took their sack lunches outside and sat on the crumbling concrete steps to eat. Marie had just taken a bite of her tuna sandwich when Mr. Cline reappeared. Without a word to them he went inside. They heard him walking around the first floor, then up the stairs, and down again. When he came back out he said rather grudgingly, "You've made a fair start."

22

"Start!" Ham said. "Did you see all the junk we swept up?"

"That 'junk' is what hoodlums like you have been leaving in my house for years. It's about time you learned to respect someone else's property."

"How old is the house, Mr. Cline?" Marie wanted to change the subject quickly, before Ham's temper could get them into ever worse trouble.

"I believe Treason House was built in 1774. Now this afternoon..."

"Treason House?" David asked.

"It's always been known as Treason House."

"Why?" asked Marie.

Cline looked at her suspiciously. "What do you care about it? Just trying to delay getting back to work, aren't you?"

"No, really, I want to know why they call it Treason House." Truthfully, Marie did not care very much, but it seemed better to keep Mr. Cline talking.

"Well, Prudent Hooper, the man who built the house, was supposed to have hidden a British spy here during the War."

"You mean the Revolutionary War?" asked Marie.

"He said 1774," David told her. "What'd you think he meant, World War II?"

She ignored David. "So the guy who built this house was a traitor?"

Cline scowled at the word *traitor*. "I don't think so," he said. "Prudent Hooper was a successful fish

23

merchant. According to the stories my family told, he built this big house shortly before the Revolution. Some time during the war a mob surrounded the house and trapped this suspected spy inside. The man jumped to his death from the widow's walk, and Prudent Hooper lived with doubts about his loyalty for the rest of his days. But no one ever proved he was a traitor."

"What's a widow's walk?" Izzy asked.

The old man pointed to the roof, where they could see a railed-in area between the two big chimneys on either side. "They used to call that the widow's walk because sailors' wives watched the sea from there, and so often their husbands never did come home alive."

"Where'd the guy land when he jumped off the roof?" Ham asked. "Can you see the bloodstain or anything?"

"That was two hundred years ago," Cline said.

David had one more question. "What's a phrenologist?"

"You mean old Reginald Galusha? Oh, they used to think you could tell a lot about a person by studying the bumps on his head. Galusha rented this house back about 1922, when I was away in the service. I suppose he's the last person who actually lived here." Hooper Cline turned and started to walk away. "You ought to be able to finish mopping the floors today," he said over his shoulder. "Next week you can start on the walls."

Ham stared after Mr. Cline. "Maybe you three are going to be here next week," he muttered. "I'm not."

3

On the following Friday afternoon, Marie and Isabelle went to the high-rise apartment building where both David and Ham lived. It was Izzy's idea. She thought that if all three of them talked to Ham once more, he might change his mind and continue the work on Treason House. The girls met David in the main lobby.

"Look at the walls of this elevator," Marie said as she pushed the button for the eighth floor. "Somebody should do something about all this vandalism."

Dave snorted, but Isabelle nodded seriously. The grimy beige walls of the self-service elevator were covered with all sorts of messages, phone numbers and initials written with everything from ball point pens to lipstick.

"This isn't going to do any good," Dave said as the elevator clanked up. "I know Schmidt, and he told me just this morning he wasn't going out to that house again."

"We have to try," Izzy insisted.

"Anyway, four can get done faster than three. Even if Ham isn't much help, he's better than nobody." Marie made a face when the door slid open. "This hall stinks."

"You'd get used to it if you lived here, Miss Delicate," Dave said angrily, and Marie remembered that his family had only moved into the Oceanside Apartments that fall. He probably didn't like it. It wasn't really such a bad building; in fact it looked nice from the outside, all white and modern. But the hall did smell.

Marie stumbled over a broken tricycle some kid had left beside the elevator and landed painfully on one knee. "Watch where you're going," David told her. "Come on, it's this way. 807."

Mrs. Schmidt let them in. She was a big woman with dark blonde hair braided and wound around her head. "Arnie's in there," she said when she saw David, indicating the next room with a jerk of her thumb. Without paying any more attention to them she went back to the game of solitaire that was laid out on a card table by the window.

They found Ham stretched out in front of the television set, still in his pajamas.

"I'm not going out there tomorrow," he said immediately, and went on watching the cartoon.

"Mr. Cline will tell the judge if you don't show up," David told him.

"So what?"

"I don't think they'll let you watch TV much at reform school," said Marie.

"Oh, buzz off," Ham said. "My Dad can take care of that judge, and old Cline too. Nobody gets sent to reform school the first time they're picked up. He was just trying to scare us."

David brushed his black hair out of his eyes and looked down at Ham disgustedly. "You goof-off, you're just too lazy to do your share. I hope Mc-Gruder sends you up for twenty years. You heard him say he's starting a new get-tough policy with vandals. What was it, ten thousand dollars the city spent just fixing broken windows last year?"

"Well, I never broke ten thousand dollars worth of windows. I didn't do that much harm to Cline's old wreck, either. You guys can blister your hands out there all summer if you want to . . ."

"We're supposed to do it together," Isabelle reminded him.

They heard the front door slam, and Will Schmidt strode in with two of his friends. They were wearing sweaty baseball shirts and carrying their gloves.

"Well, well," Ham's brother said, grinning. "The little boys and girls are having a meeting."

27

Ham seemed to shrink, and Marie was surprised to find she felt sorry for him. "Let us alone," he mumbled.

"How're you coming on your cleanup project?" Will asked. He turned to his buddies. "Do you know the cops have my brilliant brother and his friends fixing up that old wreck on Orchard Lane? Seems they got caught with a lot of wicked vandals making a mess out there."

One of Will's friends, a tall, flabby boy Marie thought had been at the house that night, shook his head with mock disapproval. "Naughty, naughty!"

Ham got up, his face pink with anger. "You'd be working out there too, if . . ."

"If I was as dumb as my little brother."

"Now, William," Mrs. Schmidt's voice came tiredly from the next room.

"You kiddies having lots of fun out there?" Will asked, ignoring his mother.

"It's no so bad," Ham said. "I don't mind."

Marie tried not to look surprised. She'd expected him to announce to his brother that he was quitting. But she guessed all he wanted right now was to say the opposite of anything Will said. She remembered a few fights like that, before her older sister had left home for good. "I've got to go," she told no one in particular, and edged toward the door.

David followed, throwing one last, annoyed look at Ham.

"See you in the morning," Isabelle called as they went out into the hall.

Marie did not realize how late it was until they passed the corner drugstore with the big clock in the window. "Yipes," she said to Izzy, "it's after six!"

Loreen Bellotti stood in the doorway, watching. Marie saw her mother and pumped hard down the last half-block to her house. "Sorry," she called breathlessly, "I didn't notice how late it was."

"Where have you been?" Marie was mystified by the harsh tone of Mrs. Bellotti's voice; it wasn't as late as all that.

"We went over to Schmidt's, at the Oceanside Apartments. Didn't I tell you?"

"No. You just said you were going somewhere with Izzy. The Oceanside is halfway downtown."

"Oh, Mom, it's just a little way beyond school." Marie plopped into a chair in the kitchen and fanned herself. "Whew, it's hot out. Is there any lemonade?"

"You simply have to be more careful about letting me know where you're going, and getting home on time, Marie." Mrs. Bellotti went to the stove and began stirring something in a saucepan. Marie noticed the tight lines around her mouth and suddenly realized that was the matter.

"You don't trust me any more, do you?"

"It isn't a matter of trusting. I just . . ."

"No, you never used to get all worried when I was a few minutes late getting home. Since we got in that—that trouble, you expect me to be out doing some terrible thing every day. Don't you?"

"Of course not." Mrs. Bellotti stirred faster, not looking at Marie. "I can't follow you around every minute. I expect you to behave yourself. But, then, I never expected you to get into anything like that business at the old house, and I never expected Louise to quit school and run off to California."

"Oh, *that* again. You think I'm going to take off like she did? Good grief!"

"Would you get the salad out of the refrigerator and call your father? He's out back, clipping the hedge."

Marie did as her mother asked, feeling angry and misunderstood and a little guilty all at the same time. Her father didn't help matters by quizzing her again about why she'd been late. But at last he got started on the poor quality beef he'd been getting in the meat department of the supermarket where he worked as a butcher. Marie usually had a lot to say at meals, but tonight she was glad to let her parents talk about something besides her tardiness.

"Marie, the library is open tonight. Would you take this book back for me?" Mrs. Bellotti asked when the dishes were done.

"Well—OK." Marie had intended to watch television, but she decided she'd better do what she could to make peace. It was only a few blocks to the library, anyway.

The first person she saw when she got there was Dave Keller, hunched over a big book at a table near the door. She often ran into him at the library; it seemed like he was always reading. Marie liked to read if the story was exciting or funny. She couldn't imagine being interested in the sort of books David

read—but then he was supposed to be some kind of a brain.

"Bellotti," he whispered when he spotted her. "Come here, look at this."

"What?" she asked, leaning on the heavy wooden table.

"I've been looking up some stuff about that old house. I thought maybe I could find out more about the spy Cline told us about. See, here's what the place used to look like."

There was a photograph of Treason House, not broken-down as it was now but freshly painted, with a horse and buggy in front of it. The caption said: "Hooper House. Date constructed: Unknown. Sometimes called Treason House, for obscure reasons.

Has very old painting of eagle over fireplace. Once housed a religious sect, the Nahumites. Possibly used as a station on the Underground Railroad."

"Hey, it looks different in the picture," Marie said. "With the shutters open like that, and the grass cut and everything, it's sort of neat. When was the picture taken?"

"The book was published in 1920. Some time before that, I guess." He showed her the cover, which said simply: *Old Houses of New Glasgow.*

" '. . . called Treason House for obscure reasons,' " Marie read aloud. "What's that mean?"

"It means they don't know why. Obscure: hidden, not understood . . ."

"All right, so you're a walking dictionary. But what about the story of the spy who jumped off the roof?"

"Whoever put this book together probably hadn't heard about him. But did you get that part about the Underground Railroad? Maybe there's a secret room someplace, where they used to hide slaves!"

A man at the next table was scowling at them, so Marie went back to whispering. "Where would we look for a secret room?"

"I don't know. In the attic, maybe, or there might be a trap door in the floor."

"We mopped all those floors last week, and I didn't see any trap door. Anyway, we're not going to have any time to hunt for secret rooms. We have to clean off the walls tomorrow, remember? Is Ham really going to show up?"

David nodded and closed the book. "I saw him after supper, and he said his brother's been trying to get him to quit. So now he won't. Maybe he's figured out that Will isn't as smart as he thought."

"Yeah. Well, see you in the morning."

Marie still had a quarter left from her week's allowance. After returning her mother's book at the main circulation desk, she decided to go out the side door and stop at the drive-in on Twenty-eighth Street for an ice cream cone.

On her way out she had to pass a small room that was used by the library for displays. She glanced through the door, remembering an exhibit of Egyptian mummies they'd had there once.

HERITAGE WEEK, a sign on the wall read. NEW GLASGOW COUNTY HISTORICAL SOCIETY.

The room was filled with models of houses, set up on low tables. A woman was in the corner pasting labels on some of the models.

Marie wandered in, past a table of models marked "Saltbox houses: Seventeenth Century." They didn't look much like saltboxes to her. The houses were plain and rather ugly, she thought, with steep-sloped roofs and chimneys in the middle.

Then she saw a table of models that reminded her of Treason House. "Georgian," the label said. "Late Colonial."

Each house was marked with the name of the owner and the date it had been built. Several of them had the same sort of shutters, the same "widow's walk" on the roof, the same chimney as Mr. Hooper's house. But none was exactly the same, and they were all marked with different names.

Marie studied them for a few minutes and then read the card sealed in plastic and glued to the front of the table. It said:

"Only a few dozen examples of Georgian colonial architecture remain in New Glasgow County. Each of these fine old houses is represented by a model. Tours of the Cogswell House and the Tufft House are offered each spring and fall by members of the New Glasgow County Historical Society."

Marie said, "Um, excuse me?"

The woman turned slowly and looked at Marie. She wore an expensive-looking suit, and her brown hair was twisted into an elaborate arrangement and sprayed stiff.

"I think this sign is wrong," Marie told her.

"In what way?" the woman asked, looking at Marie's faded cutoffs and sleeveless sweatshirt.

"I know of a house you don't have a model of, that's just as old as these."

"That's not likely."

"No, I'm sure it's this—ah—Georgian style. It was built just before the Revolution. Treason House, out on Orchard Lane."

The woman's mouth curved up, but the smile did not reach her eyes. "I'm Millicent Frothingham, of the New Glasgow County Historical Society, and I'm sure you don't realize the amount of work and research that went into the preparation of this display.

34

Dr. Reuther of the University authenticated each model. Now if this so-called Treason House were truly from the colonial period . . ."

"But it is!" Marie realized, too late, that she was interrupting, and decided to go on anyway. "A Mr. Hooper built the house just before the war, and a British spy committed suicide there, and that's why it's called Treason House. There's a picture of it in a book right in this library."

"Well, if you want to show me the picture, perhaps we can clear this up." Mrs. Frothingham sounded bored.

When Marie got back to the main reading room, David was gone. She'd already forgotten the exact title of the book, and hadn't noticed the author's name. She considered leaving by the other door, but could not give up that easily.

"I couldn't find it," she said rather lamely when she got back to the display room. "My friend had already turned it in. There really is such a house, though."

"And how do you happen to know about it? Is it yours?"

"Well, no. I've been sort of helping to clean it up."

"My dear, your interest in history is commendable." Mrs. Frothingham smiled slightly. "Our society has some lovely coloring books that depict the history of this region. I'd be glad to leave one for you if you'd pick it up here in the next few days."

"I don't want a coloring book." Marie was mad now. Her words tumbled out with no thought at all,

and her face felt hot. "I just thought you might want to know about the house, that's all. It's built just like these, with the same kind of door and chimney and everything, even that rail around the roof."

Her hands moved as she drew Treason House in the air with her fingers.

"Many houses used the same general plan." The smile was gone, and Mrs. Frothingham spoke sharply, like a teacher ordering somebody to the principal's office. "The techniques for establishing the age of a building are much too complicated for me to explain. You'd better just go on home now, young lady."

"All right, but it really is old," Marie said stubbornly. "It even has the same exact shutters as that one." Her right hand thrust out to point to a model at the back of the table, and caught the corner of another one near the edge. The model crashed to the floor and fell apart.

4

"Look what you've done, you careless girl!" Mrs. Frothingham stooped to pick up the pieces of the broken model.

"I'm sorry, it was an accident," said Marie miserably, trying to help. "Look, this wall could be glued back on, and the steps . . ."

"I'll have to see whether it can be repaired. You just go on, now, before you break something else."

By the time she got home and finished eating her double chocolate marshmallow delight cone, Marie did not feel quite so unhappy. She hadn't intended to break the thing, after all. Maybe she had let her temper run away with her—but that woman from the Historical Society had been pretty rude, too. The way she'd acted, they ought to call it the Hysterical Society! Anyway, Marie would probably never see Mrs. Frothingham again.

They were all at the house by nine the next morning. Dave had something to show them when they met on the front steps: a yellowed scrap of newspaper with a picture of a skull on it, like the one on the sign beside the door. "Reginald Galusha, Phrenologist," it said. "Your character analyzed, your future predicted. Monday-Friday, 8-5. Evenings by appointment. 4214 Orchard Lane, New Glasgow."

"I was telling my Pop about this place, and he found this clipping in the morgue," Dave told them.

"Morgue?" asked Izzy.

"That's what they call the basement at the newspaper, where they store all the old papers and file clippings. Pop works there," Dave explained. "Most of the stuff is on microfilm, now, but there's still a room full of file folders on different subjects. This was in a file on fortune tellers and people like that who used to live in New Glasgow."

"I wonder if old Galusha had to shave your head before he'd tell your fortune," Marie said, looking at the bald head in the picture and fingering her long, black hair.

"He wouldn't have many customers with *that* kind of requirement," said David. "But then people must have been pretty dumb in those days, to believe in this phrenology stuff."

"My sister won't date a fellow without checking

39

his horoscope," Isabelle commented.

Ham stood on the top step in front of the door and put his hands on Dave's head. "What's this? An absolutely smooth skull. Why sir, I don't know how to tell you this—your head is just one big bump!"

Hooper Cline came limping around the corner of the house, and they all went silent as he unlocked the door. He showed them buckets of soapy water, sponges, rags and brushes for cleaning the walls. He opened the shutters on the ground floor to give them more light, and set up two stepladders in the hallway so they could reach to the high ceilings.

They looked at the walls, grimy with years of dirt, splattered with spray paint and dried shaving cream, cracked and peeling in many places.

"We'll never get these clean," Marie groaned.

"It won't hurt you to try," Cline said coldly. "You and your friends had fun making this mess. Now you'll know what it takes to undo that sort of entertainment."

The front hall had been papered with a greenish wallpaper covered with pink roses. The colors had faded until the pattern was almost impossible to recognize, unless you looked very closely. Marie pulled idly at a loose piece, and it came off in her hand.

"It might be easier to peel off the wallpaper than to try to get it clean," she said.

"Probably so. Do that if you want to," Hooper Cline said. Marie thought it was strange that he didn't care what they did to the house as long as they learned the grim lesson he wanted to teach them. To put off the job a few more minutes, she decided to see what he would say about her encounter with Mrs. Frothingham.

"There's a display of colonial houses at the library," she said, "but they don't have a model of Treason House."

Cline shrugged.

"I tried to tell this lady from the Historical Society about it, and she insisted I was wrong, that it wasn't really built before the Revolution."

"This house was built in 1774 or 1775," Mr. Cline said.

"I found a picture of it in a book about old houses in New Glasgow," David said. "But it had 'unknown' after 'date constructed.'"

"Books, historical societies—what's the difference?" Mr. Cline sounded angry. "Nobody cares about that sort of thing these days. Newer, bigger, better, faster, that's all that matters. Get started on those walls."

He left them, and Marie sighed and picked up a bucket. "Let's try the sponges first," she suggested. "Maybe if we get the paper wet it'll peel off easier."

Ham had to try scooping water in a tin can and throwing it at the walls, but that way it didn't soak in well enough and too much was wasted on the already-clean floors. Gradually they worked out a system, the girls going over the walls with sponges and the boys peeling paper. In the front hall they exposed bare, crumbling plaster. After they got past the doors to the front rooms they began to find old

41

newspapers under the wallpaper.

" 'Scrawny Babies need Scott's Emulsion,' " Ham read from an ad. " 'It brings the dimples back.' "

"Look at the grocery prices," Izzy said. "Eggs, 12¢ a dozen. Butter, 18¢ a pound. Sugar, a hundred pounds for five dollars."

" 'Bryan Nominated by Democrats in Chicago,' " Dave read from a headline. "There's a date on this— 1896."

Marie found a sentimental poem and peformed it loudly, with sighs and dramatic gestures:

> Oh, thou beloved, who shouldst have been mine own,
> Serenely beautiful and wise and strong,
> Too late! Too late! the darkness gathereth,
> And the night falleth, pitiless and dumb;

"Dumb is right," commented Dave.

> I cannot reach thee with this hopeless breath;
> But when I walk the other side of death,
> Wilt thou not come?

Marie collapsed in a heap on the floor and played dead until Ham drizzled water from his sponge on her head.

Now they all ripped off the old wallpaper eagerly so that they could read the newspapers underneath. Izzy found an article that labeled the woman's suffrage movement "a gigantic joke and an insult to the purity of the gentle sex." Ham uncovered some old drawings of plains Indians and one of a horseless carriage that could cover almost ten miles in an hour. Dave was delighted with the announcement of a play called *Blue Jeans* in which the hero was threatened by "a real, operating buzz saw" in "the sawmill scene."

"The Delusion Mouse Trap" pictured an elaborate cagelike structure that was supposedly "filling up the little mouse cemeteries throughout the land at an appalling rate."

"Do you think people really *bought* those things?" Marie asked.

"Just imagine how weird some of our TV commercials will sound in a hundred years," Dave said.

"Yeah, imagine a bunch of space dudes getting a look at one of those mouthwash ads. They'd think everybody in this century had a permanent case of bad breath," said Ham.

"And sour stomach, and headache, and tired blood," added Isabelle.

By noon they had most of the wallpaper off in the hall, and had started on the large front room with the elaborate brick fireplace. The work went faster there, because the walls were simply painted plaster and could be sponged off quickly. They were done with the room when they stopped to eat lunch.

It was hot and muggy outside. They decided to stay in the house, and sat in a semi-circle around the empty fireplace.

"Tuna sandwich again," Marie complained when she opened her sack. "Does anybody want to trade? What do you have, Izzy?"

"Peanut butter. I'll trade if you want."

44

"No, I got sick of peanut butter sandwiches carrying my lunch to school all year. What's yours, Ham?"

"Ham."

"I might have known. Want to trade?"

"Nope."

"Don't look at me," said David. "I didn't bring a sandwich. Two hard-boiled eggs and a pepperoni pizza, see?"

"Cold pizza? Yuck! I guess I'll just have to eat the tuna sandwich." Marie spread her lunch out on a folded newspaper and looked for something else she might trade for dessert; her mother was on a health kick and thought she ate too many sweets.

"I wonder if that bird's really two hundred years old." Dave said, looking at the painting over the fireplace.

Even though the paint was faded and the background soiled with soot, it was an impressive picture. The eagle's wings spread over the entire length of the mantel, probably six feet or more. His head was cocked to one side, and his beady eye seemed to look right out into the room. Clutched in his talons was what looked like a bundle of sticks.

"That must be the picture that was mentioned in that book you showed me at the library," Marie said.

Dave nodded. " '. . . very old painting of eagle,' it said. We probably ought to wash that off, too."

"Terrific," said Ham. "Now he's thinking up more work for us to do!"

Isabelle got up and ran her fingers over the painting. "I don't think we ought to use water on it," she said. "Look, the paint is sort of cracked and chipped. We might ruin it."

"Yeah, let's get on to the next room," Marie said, wadding up her bread crusts and stuffing them back into the sack. "I have to get home in time to clean up *my* room or I can't go to the movies tonight."

The doors in the house were all quite low. Dave hopped over a discarded broom and banged his head as he left the room.

"Too bad Reginald Galusha isn't around any more," Ham told him. "You're going to have a beautiful bump there in a minute."

Dave ducked through and rubbed his forehead. "This house must've been built by midgets," he grumbled.

"I read somewhere that everybody used to be shorter in the olden days," said Marie. "Something to do with what they ate. I guess they didn't have pepperoni pizza and hard-boiled eggs."

The next room also had a fireplace, but it was smaller and there was no painting over it. It was papered like the hallway, and again the ancient wallpaper hung in shreds and tatters. Somebody had written LOUIS J. IS A FINK across one wall with spray paint.

Instead of old newspapers, they found another layer of wallpaper under the first. It was a sort of yellowish color with a different floral pattern, and it was rotting and peeling just like the top layer. Both came off easily to reveal still another layer of paper, a plain blue.

They worked as quickly as they could, ripping off hunks of wet wallpaper and tossing them into the pasteboard box they had put in the middle of the room. Sometimes the paper clung stubbornly to the wall. They had to leave patches of yellow or green in places, and even where they got down to the blue it was streaked with water and bits of old paste.

"Do you think Mr. Cline's going to like the looks of this room?" Marie asked, standing back to look at the long wall they'd finished.

"It's got to be better than 'LOUIS J. IS A FINK,'" Dave said.

Isabelle nodded. "And he did say we could peel off the old wallpaper."

Ham threw a wad of wet paper at Marie. It hit the side of her face, and she picked it up and hurled it back at him. Laughing, he ducked and grabbed another piece from the waste box. Marie snatched a hunk from the wall and let fly before she saw Hooper Cline appear in the doorway behind Ham.

Ham ducked, and Marie's paperwad hit Mr. Cline in the chest. She froze when she saw him. Ham noticed the looks on the faces of the other three and turned around to face the owner of Treason House.

Cline did not say anything, but his heavy black eyebrows drew together. He bent over slowly and picked up the paperwad from the floor.

"Gee, I'm sorry, Mr. Cline," Marie stammered. "We really have been working until just now. We finished the hall and the room next door and we've

47

got one wall done in here, see?"

Isabelle was still standing near the wall and was picking nervously at the scraps of paper clinging to it. This was a section they had not cleaned yet. A bit of the bottom layer came off in her hand, and she suddenly exclaimed, "Look!"

Glad of the diversion, they all crowded around and saw a face about the size of a fist peering out at them from beneath the ancient wallpaper.

"What's that, more old newspapers?" Ham asked.

"No, it's in color," said Dave. "Anyway, it doesn't look like paper. It's some sort of a painting."

"Be careful!" Mr. Cline said as they began pulling and scraping at the paper around the face. He looked at the wall, then reached out with one bony finger to touch it. "I remember my grandfather saying that some of the walls were decorated with frescoes when the house was first built."

"What's a fresco?" Marie asked.

"It's a painting, done on wet plaster instead of canvas. I always assumed they painted over all those old pictures. Bring me a sponge."

He daubed gently around the face, pulling off the wallpaper as they watched. After about fifteen minutes he'd exposed the figure of a young man dressed in eighteenth-century knee breeches with some sort of pack on his back. He was looking back over his shoulder, and his long hair was tied at the neck with a string. Behind him was a large house that looked very much like Treason House. An older man stood in the doorway pointing in the direction the young

48

man was going.

Hooper Cline studied the painting for a few moments with a strange look on his face. Then he dropped the sponge into a bucket of water and limped out of the room. "You ought to have time to do the stairway wall before you leave," he called back to them.

"Wow, Izzy, you saved us by finding that face," Marie said when he was gone. "I wonder what this picture is supposed to be, anyway?"

"The young guy just enlisted in the army," Dave suggested. "His father's telling him to go blast those redcoats."

"No," said Marie, "he's just announced he's going to backpack through the colonies. His father's yelling, 'You and your long-haired weirdo friends ought to stay and help on the farm instead of running around singing Yankee Doodle!' "

" 'And don't come back 'til you've got a job!' " Ham added.

"Speaking of jobs," Dave said, "we'd better get at that stairway wall or we'll be here all night. Why don't you girls finish up in here, and we'll start on that."

"Yeah, let them do the easy stuff," Ham grumbled, following Dave back to the hall.

Marie and Isabelle found a little more background to the painting as they finished cleaning the wall, but no more figures. The last wall in that room was simply plaster under the blue paper. They worked fast, soaking the surface with water and then pulling off soggy chunks of old wallpaper. Water from the sponge trickled down Marie's arm as she reached for the high sections.

They were almost done with the room when they heard Dave yelling in the hallway: "Izzy! Marie! C'mere, look what we found. A waterfall!"

5

It gushed down the wall along the stairway, beginning with a peaceful-looking river at the landing and ending at the foot of the stairs with a tremendous explosion of spray.

"Looks real enough to swim in," David said when they had the whole thing exposed. There were only two layers of wallpaper over it, and those were old and loose enough to peel off easily.

"That's cool, the way it runs down beside the stairs." Marie touched the waterfall with her hand and then looked at her fingers, as if she expected them to be wet.

"Hey, there's fish down here!" Ham pointed to the

51

pool at the bottom, and sure enough there were shadowy fish-shapes under the water and one leaping into the air.

"Let's see what it looks like from back here," Izzy suggested, moving toward the front entrance.

They followed her and stood in the shadowy doorway.

There was a large window on the stairway landing. Through its broken panes the sunlight poured on the waterfall, making it seem almost real. With no banister the stairs hung like a long, curving path beside it.

"This must've been some house, in the old days," Dave said softly.

The front door opened and they heard Hooper Cline's gruff voice behind them. "You still here?" Then he saw what they were looking at. He limped through the hall and stood at the foot of the stairs.

Marie expected him to smile for once, to show at least as much interest as the four of them. After all, it was his house. But he only looked grumpier than ever. And all he said was, "It's after five."

"After *five*?" Dave yelped.

"We're supposed to be through at four," Ham said.

Mr. Cline helped them pick up the sponges and scrub brushes. "I assumed you'd already left," he told them. "You can quit an hour earlier next week, if you want to."

"No, this way we've worked an extra hour," Marie said. "We'll get the hundred hours done that much faster. Let's see, eight hours last week, nine today, that's seventeen hours . . ."

"Only eighty-three to go," Dave said.

"That's just great." Ham scowled, his temporary interest in the waterfall forgotten. "Let's go home."

Marie half expected Ham to back out again, but he was there the next Saturday morning. It was hot and still, one of those summer days when the air seems almost too thick to breathe. Marie noticed a clump of black clouds piling up in the distance just before they went inside.

They finished washing the downstairs walls that morning. There were only two more rooms to do; a large back room that had obviously been the kitchen, and a square front room that they dubbed the Torture Chamber because of a peculiar object they found there.

It was an iron thing as tall as a man with many-pointed branches sticking out on each side and a small mirror toward the top. Most of the "arms" stuck out to the right and left, but one pair curved back like giant handcuffs.

It was Ham who decided the thing was an instrument of torture. "See, they'd strap your legs in this gadget down here," he said, "and then tie your arms out on these deals . . . "

". . . and you'd have to look at yourself in the mirror all day," finished Marie. "Wow, that would be torture!" She climbed into the iron loops, draped her arms over the branches and made a face in the mirror.

"C'mon, Bellotti, let's get started on the walls," Dave said.

No more paintings turned up under their efforts,

but they did find more old newspapers under the kitchen wallpaper behind a black cast-iron stove that still stood in that room. They were reading the advertisements when they heard someone come in the front door and through the hall. The steps were firm and fast, so they knew it could not be Mr. Cline. A tall policeman appeared in the kitchen doorway.

"All right," he said in a tired voice, "what're you kids up to?"

Izzy went pale, Ham glared at the policeman defiantly, and David slouched against the wall as if he'd been caught in some crime.

"Let's have your names and addresses," the policeman ordered, taking out a little tablet and a pencil.

"Wait a minute," Marie said, much too loudly. "We're not doing anything wrong. We're cleaning up these walls for the man who owns the house."

"Just a little summer job, eh?" the man asked. "I happen to know this place has been deserted for years. We check it regularly, and about once a month a bunch of kids break in and tear it up."

"But..."

"Forget it, Marie," Ham said. "He's not going to believe us."

At that moment Hooper Cline walked in. It was the first time Marie had ever been glad to see him. He had an old-looking black book in one hand and a brown paper bag in the other. "What's the trouble?" he asked the policeman.

"You the owner?"

"That's right. My name's Hooper Cline."

"Well, I was checking the house and heard voices back here. I found these kids pulling the wallpaper off."

"It's all right. They're working for me." Surprisingly, Cline said nothing about the vandalism or Judge McGruder's sentence.

"OK. As long as you know what's going on."

After the policeman left, Cline surprised them again by opening his paper sack and handing each of them a huge apple. "It's hot today," he mumbled; I thought they might taste good."

They were good—sweet, and crisp, and cool. While the four munched their apples, Hooper Cline wandered back into the hall. They found him there later with his black book open, looking at the waterfall fresco.

"Is there something in that book about the pictures?" David asked him.

"Hm? Oh, yes. This is a journal my grandfather kept. I haven't read it for years, but I remembered him talking about a waterfall by the stairs. Here's what he says: 'Every morning when I come downstairs, I look at the waterfall and it reminds me I am home. But in the night I hear the guns again, and I forget . . .' "

"What's that mean?" Ham asked.

"My grandfather, Samuel Hooper, fought in the Civil War. After he came home he was never quite right again. In the spring he'd just disappear and they'd find him wandering around the Gettysburg battlefield. 'Shell shock,' they used to call it."

"That's spooky," Marie said.

"There's another reference to the paintings earlier, before he went to the war. Here, I've got it marked. It's dated June 12, 1859: 'Professor Slye of the University looked at our frescoes once, before Father had them papered over. The Professor thought they were probably done before Independence. The eagle is certainly of colonial times. But why it was painted as it was, or what the exact origin of the name Treason House, he could not say. I'd like to rid our family of that slander once and for all. I suspect some of our neighbors have kept the term alive because of Father's activities with the Underground Railroad.' "

"Say, there was something about that in the book I read at the library," David said. "Was this house really a station on the Underground Railroad?"

"I always heard that they hid escaped slaves here and then sent them on to Canada."

"Gee, Mr. Cline," said Marie, "when the place is cleaned up again you should have tours or something, like they do in those other old houses."

Cline snapped the book shut suddenly, and his mouth set in a hard line again, as if he'd remembered something very unpleasant. He glanced at his wristwatch and told them to start on the upstairs walls when they finished the kitchen.

"Oh, no," Ham groaned. "I'm sick of washing walls!"

The others agreed. "My arms ache, and all my fingernails are broken off," Marie told Mr. Cline.

"Isn't there something else we could do today?" Isabelle asked.

Hooper Cline looked at them and sighed. "I suppose you could work in the yard this afternoon," he said, not seeming to care very much what they did. "Come on, I'll open the tool shed and get out the mower and scythe."

David pushed the mower back and forth across what had once been the front lawn, making the rusty blades whirr through the tall, patchy grass. Marie and Izzy pulled at the weeds in the overgrown flower beds while Ham cut down the tallest of the weeds in back with a scythe.

It was hot, hard work, and soon Marie wished they'd done the upstairs walls instead. Her hands were sore and her fingers stung with grass cuts. Mosquitoes whined in her ears and chewed her neck.

Once she looked up and saw Ham standing in front of the house, staring at the door.

"Quit daydreaming and get to work, Schmidt!" she yelled furiously. "Let's get this yard done today."

"All right, all right. I was just wondering what that stain is over the front door. Looks like there was something glued up there—see?" He pointed to an odd-shaped dark pattern in the ancient wood, surrounded by paint chips.

"Probably a 'No Trespassing' sign or something," Marie said. "Come on, get the weeds on that side of the house."

Later, a hot wind piled up more dark clouds until the sun went under.

"It's going to rain," Ham said needlessly, and a clap of thunder announced the beginning of the storm like a drum roll at a parade.

Before they could get the tools stacked in the shed, big drops of rain were pounding down and lightning split the sky over Treason House. They closed the shutters over the broken windows on the first floor and raced inside.

Downstairs, every room seemed to have at least one shutter that was loose or broken. Gusts of rain showered in through the cracks, and the loose shutters banged and flapped in the wind.

"Let's go upstairs," Dave suggested. I noticed the shutters were real tight when we were doing the floors in that big front bedroom on the left side."

"We might as well eat lunch," Marie said, picking up her sack in the hall. "I'm starving."

The bedroom was dry, but dark. It reminded Marie of a "house of horrors" ride she had taken once at Coney Island, with the lightning flashing every few seconds and the wind whistling around the corners of the house. Her sandwich tasted like soggy cardboard.

"There's that box of things we were looking at the night we—broke in here," Izzy said, pointing to a large shadow in the corner. She walked to that part of the room and began rummaging through the box as she finished eating a cupcake. "Look, paper dolls."

"Oh, goody," Ham snickered.

Izzy spread out the contents of a smaller box on the floor. There was a doll about eight inches high with a simpering expression and one toe pointed. Her wardrobe included six elaborate gowns.

" 'Nancy Fancy,' " Marie read from the front of the box. "Boy, is she ever! How'd you like to haul those outfits around all day?"

Dave reached into the big box and pulled out a shabby stuffed bear and a wooden gun. "Maybe these were Mr. Cline's, when he was a kid."

Marie tried to imagine Hooper Cline as a little boy, but all she could picture was a wrinkled old man playing with a teddy bear. She giggled and dug deeper into the box.

"Here's a game," she said. "Looks a little like Monopoly. Only it's called—let's see—'A Game of Good Character.' "

There was a numbered spinner, and a board. The board was marked off in squares, each with a number corresponding to the numbers on the spinner. You started at "Early home life" and ended either at "Good Character" or "Downfall."

Marie twirled the spinner and got number eight, "Bad Influence, go back to Early Home Life." She spun it again and got fourteen, "Petty vices, take the downward path."

"Nice going, Bellotti," said Dave; "you just started and already the only way you can win is to get 'Reform.' "

"Oh, no, that sounds too much like Reform

School," Marie said, putting the board back in the box. "That's a pretty silly game, anyway. I wish the lights worked."

Isabelle picked up the "Nancy Fancy" doll and looked at it thoughtfully. "In the old days," she said, "like when some girl was playing with this, they didn't have any lights at all, did they?"

"Just candles, I guess," said Dave, "and fires in the fireplaces. Probably everybody went to bed real early."

"They wouldn't be staying up to watch TV!" Ham shook his head. "What a boring life. No TV, no movies, no records, no cars . . ."

"No supermarkets or refrigerators," Marie added, finishing her candy bar. "Just think, when you wanted to eat you'd have to chop some wood, start a fire, pull something out of the vegetable garden or shoot a deer, milk the cow, cook all the stuff over the fire . . ."

"And you'd have to carry water from someplace to wash the dishes," Izzy said. "They probably didn't need TV in those days; they were so busy working they didn't have any extra time anyway."

An especially loud blast of thunder rattled the loose shutters all over the house. The storm roared through the trees outside like a diesel truck making time on the freeway.

"What if the wind just blew this old place down?" Izzy asked nervously.

"It's been standing here for two hundred years," Dave reminded her. "Must be pretty well built to last that long. That apartment house we live in is only ten years old, and already the walls are cracking and the roof leaks and you can hear every time somebody across the hall blows his nose."

Marie looked around the shadowy room, aware suddenly of the numbers of rainstorms that must have washed over that house. "It's kind of strange to think of all the people who used to live here," she said. "I mean like that man who fought in the Civil War, Mr. Hooper's grandfather, wandering back to the battlefield every year. Maybe this was his room. Or the spy who jumped off the roof. He might have slept here. Or the kids who played with those toys."

"Yeah," Dave said, "and don't forget this was a station on the Underground Railroad. They used to hide runaway slaves somewhere in this house."

"I don't get that stuff," Ham said. "I mean, how could a house be a train station? Were there tunnels down below or something?"

"It wasn't *really* an underground railroad," Dave told him. "I read a book about it last year. That was just a sort of code name for people who helped slaves escape to Canada before the Civil War. The runaway slaves would be passed from one place to the next, and they called each hiding place a 'station.' "

Ham popped the plastic bag that had contained his sandwich. The noise reminded Marie that the thunder had stopped. A moment later the sun broke out and beamed through the cracks like the lights coming on at the end of a movie.

6

The next Saturday when the four arrived at Treason House the front yard, which they had left neatly trimmed and raked the week before, was littered with beer cans and paper. Looking at the mess, Marie felt sick. She glanced up at the house and wondered what they would find inside. It looked securely locked and shuttered. But then, she knew well enough how easy it was to break into.

Mr. Cline came with the key and smiled bitterly when he saw the looks on their faces. "Just a little party in the yard last night," he said.

"Did they get in?" Marie asked in a small voice.

"No, the police cruised by when they were working on one of the windows and they left rather quickly."

"Sure, nobody else would be stupid enough to get caught like we did," Ham said.

When Mr. Cline unlocked the door, Izzy brought out one of the waste boxes and began filling it with trash from the yard. The others helped, and Cline stood watching as they finished the job.

"You want us to work on walls again today?" Marie asked him when the yard was clear.

"I suppose so."

Dave had another suggestion. "I was looking at that banister last week," he told Hooper Cline, "and I think it would be pretty easy to fix. You've got plenty of tools in the shed. If you helped, I'll bet we could get it back up with just glue and a few nails. I used to help my pop in his workshop, before we moved to the apartments . . ."

"Yeah, most of it's still in one piece," Ham said, looking at the fallen banister.

Cline hesitated, and Marie thought again that he didn't seem very interested in getting his house fixed up. "Maybe this afternoon," he said finally. "I'll have to see if I have the right sort of glue. Nails might split that old wood. Well, finish those upstairs walls this morning. Let's see, how many hours have you put in here by now?"

"Twenty-five," Marie said promptly. "Three eight-hour days, plus that one afternoon we worked an hour overtime."

"Hm. Got a little more idea of respecting other

64

people's property, have you?"

Marie nodded hard and tried to look sincere and reformed.

Hooper Cline walked away without saying anything more, but when the front door closed behind him Marie said excitedly to other others: "He's going to let us off pretty soon!"

"He didn't say so," Ham scoffed.

"Yeah, but we're not going to have to put in a hundred hours out here," Marie insisted. "There's not that much more to do—even with Dave thinking up jobs for us."

"We didn't do a lot of the damage," Dave said, "but we did help break that banister. Besides, now that we've got the waterfall uncovered and the hall cleaned up it would—well, almost look like it did in the old days if we got the banister back up. Anyway, I think Marie's right for once. Old man Cline just wanted to teach us a lesson by having us work out here. If we keep working and convince him we're really trying, he won't make us work a hundred hours. Come on, let's get those upstairs walls washed."

As they walked up the stairs, Marie looked back down at the wide, empty hallway. "Y'know," she said, "there's something funny about Mr. Cline and this house. He doesn't seem to care what work we do, as long as we're punished for tearing up the place."

"Why should he?" Ham asked. "He doesn't live here anyway. Probably somebody else'll just mess it up again, like those guys that were out in the yard last night. It's a big waste of time."

The walls of the four large bedrooms upstairs were grimy but not as badly damaged as the ones on the first floor. Since they were painted plaster, there was no wallpaper to peel. They only had to be wiped with rags and sponged with soapy water.

When the girls were working on the last of the four rooms, David and Ham went to empty two buckets of dirty water and did not come back. Marie scrubbed angrily at a stain. "They probably went downtown for a hamburger," she grumbled.

A few minutes later they heard Dave yelling downstairs. The girls dropped their sponges and raced down. They found him in the front room with the picture of the eagle over the fireplace, pushing at a wooden panel that creaked slowly inward. Ham and Mr. Cline stood behind him.

"I found it!" he told the girls. "The secret room, where they hid the slaves in the days of the Underground Railroad."

"How did you know it was there?" Isabelle asked.

"I read someplace that a lot of these old houses had something called the 'Listening Room' or the 'Whispering Room' built right beside the main chimney. It was used to smoke meat, too, if you opened a little door to the chimney. I asked Mr. Cline about it when he came over to see what we were doing, and he remembered some kind of space beside this fireplace where he used to play when he was a kid."

"Then we just pushed until we found a piece of

the wall that moved," Ham added.

Marie peered over Dave's shoulder into the dark room. "Maybe that spy used it, too; the one Treason House is named for. Maybe he hid his secret papers in there."

"You won't find anything like that now," Hooper Cline told them. "I'd forgotten about that room, but my parents knew about it. Over the years someone would have found anything that was hidden there."

The panel finally opened all the way with a protesting shriek, and they all crowded in. It was disappointing; just a murky, stale-smelling chamber with a low ceiling and sooty brick walls.

"Phooey, no human skulls or gold bullion or mad scientist's laboratory," Marie said as they left the hidden room. "I like the torture chamber better."

"What?" Mr. Cline asked.

"The torture chamber. That's what we call the room across the hall, because of that—that thing in there. Oh, come on, I'll show you." She led the way across the hall and pointed to the iron object with the prongs and the mirror.

Hooper Cline's face contorted in a peculiar way, wrinkles branching out in new directions and his eyes squeezing together. Marie realized he was smiling.

"Young lady," he said, "this is a hat and umbrella rack. See, you would hang your hat on one of these hooks at the top and lean your umbrella in this bottom part. Then you could use the mirror to see that you got your hat on straight when you went out."

"I never saw anything like that," Izzy said. "It would be sort of handy."

"Except who wears hats?" asked Dave.

When they went back into the hallway, Ham was  standing there with a wooden eagle in his hands. It was dark and dusty, but still so life-like with its wings extended and its head cocked proudly that you could almost hear it screaming.

"I found it behind the door-panel, in the secret room," Ham said. He held it like a first-prize trophy. "And I know where it belongs," he added.

"Of course, I'd forgotten about that eagle,"

Cline said. "It used to be . . ."

"Over the front door." Ham marched outside with his find and held it up against the stain he had noticed the week before. The bird matched perfectly.

Ham lowered the eagle again and flicked a cobweb off its head. "I'm going to clean it up," he said, "and glue it back over the door." Marie looked at him in surprise; it was the first time she had ever heard Arnold Schmidt volunteer to do anything.

"Better not use soap and water on that," Mr. Cline said. "I've got some wood cleaner and oil that would be better. See, it was whittled out by hand. It must be almost as old as the painting over the fireplace."

"Hey," said David, "it does look a lot like the eagle in the picture. Maybe the same person did them both. Maybe the spy—didn't you say he was decorating the house?"

Cline nodded. "That's the legend. I don't know whether any of those pictures you found on the walls are that old, but the man who jumped off the roof was supposed to have been a sort of wandering artist. The house was new, and he was hired to do some kind of 'ornamentation.' He could have carved this."

After lunch Mr. Cline brought tools, glue and wood cleaner. He and David began working on the banister while Ham cleaned the eagle and the girls washed the few unbroken windows. Later in the afternoon Ham helped with the banister, and when it was time to leave, the long, gleaming shaft of wood was in place again.

"You can't even tell it was broken," Dave said.

"It looks fine," the old man conceded, "but it's weak in the spot we fixed. It'd never stand another bunch of kids sliding down it."

Isabelle turned to him, and her soft brown eyes studied his face curiously. "Why don't you live here? Then people wouldn't be breaking in all the time."

"Don't be too sure. Besides, it's not modern, it would cost too much to fix it up . . ." Cline's voice trailed off, and for a moment he seemed uneasy. Then he spoke briskly again. "I've got some cans of dark green paint, bought 'em on sale months ago. Next week I want to have you paint the shutters. You've done all right so far, and if you do a good job of that—well, we'll see. You can go home now."

For the first time since the night of the Carnival, Marie felt happy with herself and could think about the future without dreading it. She was sure that Hooper Cline was about to let them off and tell the Court that they had "paid their debt." She went home that night convinced that the coming Saturday would be her last at Treason House.

It was a boring week. Eileen Bernstein had a slumber party on Tuesday night, but after that there seemed to be nothing at all to do. Everyone Marie knew either had a summer job or was at the beach or out of town. On Thursday she called Isabelle to see whether she wanted to bike out to Lake Lenore and go swimming, but Izzy had to babysit with her three younger sisters.

The house kept popping into Marie's thoughts that

week. She doodled eagles on the telephone pad, piled her hair on her head and posed in her mirror as an eighteenth-century lady, even looked up "Underground Railroad" in the encyclopedia. There was nothing in the article that Dave had not already told them. The days were so long and dull that she found herself looking forward to Saturday.

Friday morning she went to the library to find something to read. Dave was there again; she half suspected that he lived at the library and slept on some dusty shelf. She drifted by his table and peeked over his shoulder at the yellowed pages of he book he was reading.

"It's about the Nahumites," he told her.

"The who?"

"Nahumites. Remember, that other book I found said that Treason House was once headquarters for a religious sect called the Nahumites. I looked 'em up in this book; its called *Religion in Nineteenth Century Connecticut*. Guess what? The whole thing was started by Lemuel Hooper, Mr. Cline's great-grandfather. The members used to live in Treason House."

"Like a monastery or something?"

"Yeah, I guess so. They based the whole religion on the Book of Nahum in the Bible."

"Never heard of it."

"Nahum's one of the prophets; it's only a couple of pages long. Anyway, it must talk about the rain and thunder and stuff, because these Nahumites only had worship services in the middle of thunderstorms. They'd go right out with the lightning zonking all over the place and sing and shout on top of some hill."

"So what'd they do all winter?"

"They were also abolitionists. That was the time when Treason House was part of the Underground Railroad."

"I get it. They spent the summer singin' in the rain and the winter hiding runaway slaves."

"Something like that. Look, here's a picture of old Lemuel Hooper."

Except for Lemuel's long beard, it might almost have been a picture of Hooper Cline. The man's fierce dark eyes were the same, and his shaggy eyebrows and strong nose.

"I'll bet they weren't too popular with the neighbors," Marie said.

"You know it. Just before the Civil War broke out, some people from New Glasgow tarred and feathered six of the Nahumites. Then all the men joined the Union Army and their wives and kids moved out, and the whole religion sort of fell apart. Says here there never were more than two dozen members."

"It still must have been pretty crowded if they all lived in Treason House."

"I guess there used to be several smaller houses nearby. Maybe the one Mr. Cline lives in is one of them."

"Yeah. Well, I've got to find a book. See you in the morning."

"See you."

There was a truck parked in front of Treason

72

House when the four of them arrived the next morning. Two men stood in the yard, looking at the house and talking. Their voices were loud, and they paid no attention to the kids parking their bicycles on the lawn.

"What do you think, a couple of days?" asked one man.

"No more than that," said the other. "Shouldn't take long to knock it down and bulldoze the land level —although some of these old places are pretty well built. Better allow three days."

7

Marie could not keep still when the meaning of the men's conversation became clear. "Excuse me," she said to them, "but are you talking about tearing down this house?"

The man who had spoken first looked down at her with a bored expression. His face was sunburned, and he wore his gray hair shaved so short that he appeared to be almost bald. "Why do you want to know?" he asked her.

"Well, we've been working here. For the owner."

"You won't be working here much longer. New city airport's going in right over there. All the buildings in this area have to go." He turned his back on her and began scribbling in a notebook.

The front door of Treason House opened and Hooper Cline came out, followed by another man who was carrying a briefcase. When he saw the four vandals standing in the yard, Mr. Cline stared at them for a moment and then looked away.

"You made us do all that work for nothing," David said.

"Not for nothing," said Mr. Cline. "To show you something about responsibility. To see that you made up for what you did."

The three strangers watched them curiously.

"Mr. Cline, you knew all along that they were going to tear down Treason House!" Izzy sounded more bewildered than angry.

"And it didn't matter whether the floors were swept or the walls were clean or anything," added Marie. "Even the stuff we did that night didn't matter, because the house won't *be* here in a few weeks."

"Oh, yes, that mattered," Cline insisted. "You didn't know the house was going to be torn down. It didn't belong to you, and yet you came in and . . ."

"How can they just wreck a place like that?" Ham asked suddenly, looking at the eagle he'd glued back over the front door. "I mean, it's been there two hundred years, and all of a sudden New Glasgow needs a bigger airport and that's the end of it."

Marie was surprised that Ham, who had dragged his feet all along and had once called Treason House " a creepy old pile of firewood," seemed to care now about what happened to it. And yet she realized that he spoke for all of them. Mad as she was about Hooper Cline's deception, she was even more upset by the thought of the bulldozers and graders that would soon flatten the old house.

"These things happen all the time," the man with the briefcase explained with sickening kindness. "It's the price of progress. Sentimental values can't stand in the way of necessity. Some day you kids will come to our fine new airport . . ."

"And park your car where Treason House used to be." Hooper Cline spoke softly, but Marie heard the bitterness in his voice. It must have been hard for him, she realized, knowing the house would be gone soon. She was not quite so angry with him.

"Let's get on with it," the red-faced man said calmly.

As the three strangers moved together and started talking about schedules and equipment, Hooper Cline walked back into the house, motioning for the vandals to follow him.

Inside, it was dark and cool. Marie looked at the stairway with its graceful banister and the waterfall following the curve of the stairs.

"A parking lot?" she said.

"I tried to convince them to leave the house," Mr. Cline said tiredly. "But then a lot of the property owners in this part of town were unhappy. They have to put the airport somewhere. And when I'm gone there won't be anyone to take care of Treason House anyway."

"This Historical Society saved other old houses around New Glasgow," David said. "I've been in a couple of 'em and they weren't half as fancy as this one."

Marie rubbed the calluses on her palm. "When I think of all the time we worked here—thirty-three hours, to be exact—and we got it looking pretty good, too . . ."

"That's why I called you in here." Mr. Cline rubbed a hand over his jaw and looked at each of them in turn. "I've written a letter to Judge Mc-Gruder, telling him that as far as I'm concerned you've worked off your obligation to me. I expect in a day or two he'll let your parents know you've served your sentence. As far as I'm concerned you can go home now; you're free."

"Yippee!" Ham yelled.

Dave tossed his sack lunch in the air and caught it again, spilling a bag of potato chips in the process. "No more getting up early on Saturday mornings."

Isabelle smiled her shy smile and remembered to thank Hooper Cline for letting them go. "I really didn't mind cleaning this place up," she said. "It was sort of fun."

The others groaned at that, but Marie had to admit to herself that the sentence had not been as bad as she had feared. And now it was all over.

They peddled home in high spirits.

When Marie and Isabelle turned into their own block, Marie looked at the six small, identical houses on each side of the street. They were all made of the same brown brick, all had the same number of windows, the same front door, the same four steps up to the door.

She waved goodbye to Izzy and parked her bike behind the house, locking it carefully because bikes were always being stolen. Inside, her mother was watering the plants in the living room. "You're home already?" Mrs. Bellotti asked in a startled voice.

"Guess what, we're all done! Mr. Cline wrote to the judge and said we'd worked enough as far as he was concerned. Anyway, the house is going to be torn down soon."

"That's wonderful."

"Not exactly, Mom." Marie flopped on the sofa and fiddled with a tassel on the souvenir pillow her father had bought at Atlantic City several years before. "I mean, they're going to wreck that old house to make room for a parking lot for the new airport. After we found those old pictures and everything. Besides, it was pretty sneaky of Mr. Cline to make us clean the place up when he knew all along it was going to be torn down."

"But at least it's all over," her mother said. "You'll be discharged by the Court."

"Yeah, I guess so. The slaves are free. We should be getting an Emancipation Proclamation from the judge any day now."

"I wish you wouldn't treat it so lightly, dear. You were in serious trouble."

"Oh, Mom, I know."

Marie called Eileen Bernstein, but she was at her cousin's for the weekend. Steph Felluccio was helping out at her parents' restaurant for the summer. Reva Lopez had broken her leg in two places. Beth La Camera had moved to Hartford.

Marie sat in the living room, brushing her hair and listening to the same record over and over. Her mother turned down the volume three times, finally gave up and went to do the grocery shopping. The phone rang.

"What're you doing?" David Keller asked.

"Oh, nothing. Isn't it great to do nothing for a change?"

"Yeah. But I've been thinking about Treason House. I don't think a place like that should be just —squashed. Those old frescoes, the stairway, the secret room, the roof that spy jumped off. None of that can ever be replaced."

"I know, but there's nothing we can do about it. Mr. Cline said the city has the power to take the land they need for the new airport. I guess they're paying him for it, but he has to sell it to them."

"Like, what if we talked to Judge McGruder?"

"Are you crazy? He's just about to turn us into human beings again, instead of J.D.'s. And you want to start something new with him?"

"It can't hurt to show him we're interested in the house now. Think how it'll look—four rotten vandals now trying to preserve the very house they damaged. What a fantastic change of heart!"

"My heart hasn't changed. I didn't know about the house before. Besides, we were just following along with those older kids . . ."

"Oh, let's not run all that through again, Bellotti. The point is, Judge McGruder must have some pull in this town. What do you say we talk to him, tell him about Treason House?"

Marie hesitated. It would be so much easier to forget the whole thing. They could all go back to the way things were before. She thought of Treason

80

House, empty and old and defenseless against the pressures of modern New Glasgow. Maybe she had changed a little, at that. The routine of her life before Treason House seemed curiously flat now. She would miss the place with its surprises and echoes of the past, its broken splendor.

"OK," she said finally. "I'll go along if you want to try talking to McGruder. But I bet it won't do any good. And you'd better not get us into any more trouble, or I'll spend a hundred hours making you wish you hadn't."

"I'm terrified. See if Izzy can come, and meet us at the front door of the good old Oceanside Apartments in half an hour."

"Us? You mean you've talked Ham into this wild goose chase?"

"It was his idea."

8

The New Glasgow County Court House was a new building, very modern and streamlined, five stories high. It stood in the heart of the city, having been built as part of an urban renewal project. Carved in stone over the front entrance was a quotation from Justice Oliver Wendell Holmes: "The life of the law has not been logic; it has been experience."

Walking up the wide front steps, Marie wondered whether her mother had come home yet and found her note. The note had been true as far as it went: "I'm taking the bus downtown with Izzy. Back this afternoon." Marie knew better than to mention that they planned to approach Judge McGruder with a new problem. Mrs. Bellotti had been shaken up enough by her daughter's first brush with the law.

The Court House lobby echoed with tile and empty space. Abstract designs decorated the walls and the floor. Marie remembered the chill she'd felt the first time they had been here, for the hearing on their case. She almost ran to the elevators, anxious now to get the business over with.

They got out of the silent elevator on the fourth floor and walked down the hallway to Judge McGruder's courtroom.

"Sure aren't many people around here today," Ham said nervously.

"It's Saturday," Dave reminded him. "I don't think they have trials or anything on Saturdays."

"He probably isn't even here," said Marie.

But the courtroom doors were open. The empty room looked like a movie set, all ready for the actors to appear. There were the American flag and the flag of the State of Connecticut; the jury box, the witness stand; the seats for the spectators, the judge's desk or "bench" with his gavel. Marie wanted to turn around and hurry back outside, into the sunshine.

At that moment a skinny little man came out of a side room, glaring. "What do you kids want?" he asked in a high-pitched voice.

David stepped forward. "We want to see Judge McGruder."

"Why?"

"Can't we explain to him?"

"I'm his bailiff. If you've got business with the

Judge, you can tell me first."

"It has to do with a case he had about a month ago."

"Oh, yes, I remember you." The bailiff stepped closer and squinted at them. "You're the four kids who vandalized that old house. You in trouble again?"

"No," Dave told him, "it's about the house. Really, we won't take long if you'll just let us see the Judge."

"Sorry, he's busy in his chambers. You want me to make you an appointment?"

"There isn't time for that!" David had been carefully polite, but now he could not help sounding impatient. "Just five or ten minutes . . ."

"You can't just barge in here and interrupt Judge McGruder, Sonny. If you don't want an appointment I'll have to ask you to leave."

Ham had been edging away from the group, behind the bailiff's back and toward the far side of the courtroom. Now he banged suddenly on the door to Judge McGruder's chambers.

"Say, get away from there!" barked the bailiff. But before he could cross the room the door opened and Carleton McGruder stood there.

He was a big man, not fat, but solid in his pearl-gray suit. The overhead light gleamed on his bald head.

"What's going on?" he asked. He looked directly at Ham, not over his head at the bailiff. "Let's see, you're Arnold Schmidt, right?"

"Right," Ham said. "We want to see you for just

a minute, but that guy . . ."

"It's OK, William," the Judge said to the bailiff, opening the door wider. He pulled up a big stuffed chair for each of them and sat down behind his desk. "Now, what's the problem? I had an excellent report on your work from Mr. Cline just the other day."

"Did he tell you Treason House is going to be torn down to make room for the new airport?" Marie asked him.

"Treason House? What . . ."

And then they were all talking at once, trying to explain the name and what was going to be done to the house and how they had found out.

"Wait a minute," McGruder said, holding up his hands. "Slow down, one at a time, or I'll have to have you write some more five-hundred-word essays."

"Ish!" Marie said. "You tell him, Dave."

So David told the story of Treason House, its past, the things they had found there, the facts they had learned about the history of the house, and their discovery that it was to be demolished. The Judge listened quietly, studying their faces.

Dave concluded with a speech they had planned on the bus ride to the Court House: "Judge, you and the police called us vandals because we broke some things and messed up an old house. We did what you said to make up for that. We wrote those essays and we worked hard and cleaned up a lot more than we were responsible for. What we want to know is, how can the city go out there now and destroy the whole house, just wipe it out?"

"Well, I don't know exactly what the plans are, but that's a different matter. It's necessary sometimes to sacrifice for the sake of the future. I don't see the connection with your vandalism."

"Have you still got our essays?" David asked.

The Judge nodded and took a cardboard folder out of the file cabinet behind him.

"Could I have mine, please?" Dave took the two sheets of lined notebook paper Judge McGruder handed him. "Here it is, the definition of vandalism I got from the dictionary: "Willful destruction of the beautiful.'"

"Willful destruction of the beautiful," the Judge repeated slowly. "There was an old Court House where this building stands. I always wished . . . but you see, that's the point. If we preserved all our old buildings there'd be no room for anything new."

"Sure," Marie said, unable to keep still any longer. "But when it's something really special, like Treason House, and when all they're going to put in its place is a *parking lot* . . ."

"You can't have an airport without parking space." The Judge spoke quickly, but he was beginning to sound a bit less sure. "I happen to know it took years for the planning commission to settle on that spot for the airport. There aren't many houses out there, and most of them are in poor condition."

Now even Isabelle had to speak up. "Treason House is two hundred years old," she said. "We didn't know that when we went in there. We didn't know all the things that happened there, or about the frescoes or the secret room or the eagle. The men who are planning that airport probably don't know either. But if you told them, Judge, don't you think maybe they would change their minds?"

The Judge's chambers were quiet. They could see that McGruder was thinking, and he didn't look angry. He looked at something in the cardboard folder on his desk, scribbled a note on the blotter, and picked up the telephone.

"Stan?" he said when his call got through. "This is Carl McGruder. Got a minute? Good. I have a question on that airport project. There's an old house at 4214 Orchard Lane that's to be torn down. I've just learned that it may have some rather special historial value. Is there any chance that it could be left where it is?" There was a long pause, and then the Judge said, "I see. All right, we'll check it out. I may be talking to you later."

He hung up the telephone and turned back to them. "The house is on the far edge of the planned parking lot," he said. "In theory, at least, the lot could be redesigned to leave it. But that would be expensive, and would cause a great deal of trouble. I'm afraid the chances aren't very good."

"See!" Ham exploded. "They want us to care about other people's property, and old houses and stuff, but *they* don't care!"

"Stan did say that the planning commission might consider trying to save the house," Judge McGruder went on. "But the County Historical Society would have to investigate it and verify its age and historical value. That will take time. And they're planning to start leveling the ground in a few weeks."

"We can try," Dave insisted. "Where do we find this Historical Society?"

"They have a building on the corner of Fourth and Snead," the Judge said. "It's just a few blocks from here."

"Thanks, Judge," said Dave, turning toward the door. "Come on, let's go."

Marie hung back, suddenly remembering a broken model and a woman's angry face. That Frothingham lady had been from a County Historical Society, hadn't she? And she'd scoffed at Marie's story about Treason House. "I don't think we should just walk in there," Marie said. "I mean, they're not going to pay any attention to four kids."

McGruder nodded and stood up suddenly. "You're right. How would it be if I went along with you?"

They all stared at him in surprise, and Ham blurted: "Gee, would you do that? I never thought you'd help us—I mean, after that lecture you gave us about vandalism, and how you were cracking down, well, I didn't think you liked us much."

"I didn't like what you did to that house, and I'm not sure I like what the city's going to do any better. I'll just get my hat."

It was strange, riding down in the elevator with Judge McGruder. People stared at them as they walked across the lobby. Marie wished Ham had worn socks, and that Izzy could have found a blouse that fit her instead of one that had so obviously belonged to her older sister. In fact, Marie's own shorts and top probably didn't look too good. But she pulled up her chin and kept pace with the Judge.

The New Glasgow County Historical Society was located in a tall, narrow house beside a drug store. The house looked old, and its windows were crowded with antique lamps and dishes. Inside, most of the first floor seemed to be a sort of museum.

There was a desk near the entrance, and a brown-haired woman sat behind it, writing on little cards. Marie dodged behind Dave and marveled at her bad luck; it was Mrs. Frothingham.

The woman stood up and opened her large mouth in a toothy smile. "Why, Carleton McGruder," she said, ignoring the others. "How pleasant to see you. May I help you with something?"

"Hello, Millicent. These young people and I are interested in an old house out on Orchard Lane that's about to be torn down. We're hoping that the Society will help us to preserve it, or possibly restore it as you have this building."

"I see." Mrs. Frothingham raised her eyebrows. "You served on our Board of Directors not too long ago, Carleton. I'm sure you're aware of the limits of our funds. We have to concentrate most of our efforts on saving the few colonial homes that remain . . ."

"But this is a colonial home!" Dave broke in, paying no attention to the kick Marie gave him in an effort to keep him quiet. "It was built in 1774 or 1775."

90

Mrs. Frothingham's smile faded. She glanced at David coldly and turned back to the Judge. "Our research committee has a list of all the authentic colonial-period buildings in New Glasgow County," she announced.

"Let's begin by looking at that," McGruder suggested. "The house is the old Hooper home, sometimes know as Treason House. It's at 4214 Orchard Lane."

The woman opened a drawer of the metal filing cabinet beside her desk, took out a sheet of paper, and adjusted her jeweled glasses on the bridge of her nose. "Just as I thought," she said triumphantly. "It isn't here." Then she remembered to be polite to the Judge. "I'm so sorry; perhaps we can start a file folder on this house."

"That wouldn't help a great deal, since it's about to be torn down."

"Oh, but we could take pictures first. Preserve the memory, you know. We have a photographer who does lovely work . . ."

"Could I see that list, please?" Judge McGruder held out his hand, and after a slight hesitation Mrs. Frothingham gave him the piece of paper.

As the Judge read the list, Mrs. Frothingham watched and waited. Marie tried to shrink out of sight behind Dave, but the woman looked in her direction several times and frowned in a puzzled way, as though she were trying to remember something.

"Here it is!" Judge McGruder said suddenly. "On the back, in the part marked 'Date of construction uncertain.' "

"Well, you see, I didn't read through those," Mrs. Frothingham told him. "They're merely older buildings that could possibly date back before the Revolution. But none of them have been verified, and in most cases there is some good reason for doubt. Now, some of these will be investigated by the committee in the future. The members are all volunteers, you understand, and they can't take a great deal of time . . .'"

"Treason House doesn't have any future." It was Dave again, and Millicent Frothingham glared at him without pretending to be kind and helpful.

"Do you think there might be some sort of emergency investigation in the next few weeks?" Judge McGruder asked her patiently. "Since the house is scheduled to be demolished so soon, perhaps the committee would be willing to give it priority. Then, if they think it is of historical value, they might help us persuade the planning commission to change the boundary of the new airport parking lot just enough to spare Treason House."

"Could I ask"—Mrs. Frothingham was sweet again—"what interest these children have in the house, Judge? Are they related to the owners?"

"No, they've merely been working there this summer."

Ham had been stirring restlessly and scuffing at the floor. Marie sensed his prickly mood, and she was not surprised when he spoke up in his thin, sharp voice.

"The cops caught us fooling around in the house," he told Mrs. Frothingham defiantly. "Judge Mc-Gruder made us clean the place up."

The long mouth became a thin, disapproving line. "I see. I'm a bit surprised that you'd get involved in something like this on the word of a gang of vandals, Judge . . ."

Then she looked at Marie again.

"I thought I'd seen you somewhere before. Now I remember! This—this juvenile delinquent came to me with some silly story when I was setting up our display at the library. It must have been about that same old house. And the spiteful child actually *shattered* the model of the Ridley mansion."

9

Marie chewed her tongue and kept quiet, but she looked Mrs. Frothingham in the eye. The others watched her curiously. She hadn't told them about breaking the model at the library.

"That's beside the point now," the Judge said. "We'd like to know what we'd have to do to get the Historical Society's help in saving Treason House."

"Very well." Millicent Frothingham folded her hands primly. "First we would have to see a complete written history of the house, with documentary evidence of its age, a list of the various owners and alterations that have been made. Then a committee from the Society would inspect the place. If they de-

94

cided that it was an irreplaceable dwelling of obvious worth and that it dated back before the Revolutionary War, then we would consider what might be done to preserve it."

"Thank you. I may contact you again." Judge McGruder led the way out.

On the sidewalk, with cars and taxis hurtling by and people jostling each other in the shadows of tall, sooty buildings, Treason House seemed a fragile thing, almost like a dream. It belonged to the past.

"Maybe we should just forget the whole thing," Marie said.

"Yeah, that old lady in there sure isn't going to help," Ham agreed.

Judge McGruder put on his hat and adjusted the brim. "Now, don't let her discourage you," he told them. "I've known Millicent Frothingham for years; she just needs someone to stand up to her. I don't think the rest of the Historical Society will let her bully them on this. What do you say, shall we see what we can do?"

"Sure," Dave said. "But . . ."

Judge McGruder looked at his wristwatch. "It's almost eleven-thirty now. Can you all meet me out at the house at about two? I'll call Mr. Cline and ask him to be there too. I'm anxious to see this Treason House."

Standing together at the corner bus stop, they watched him go back through the glass doors of the new Court House.

"Wow, he sure stood off that Historical woman,"

95

Marie said.

"He's going to help us," Izzy added wonderingly.

After lunch Marie had to tell her mother where she was going that afternoon. That led to explanations, questions, answers, and more questions. In Mrs. Bellotti's opinion it was none of Marie's business what the city wanted to do with Treason House, and she would be much better off to forget the whole thing. Only the fact that they had promised to meet Judge McGruder there convinced her mother to let her go.

When Isabelle and Marie arrived at two o'clock, the door was open. Ham and Dave's bikes were parked in the yard, and an orange sports car which they assumed belong to the Judge was in the driveway. It looked odd next to the ancient, silvery house.

They found the others in the large front room, with Dave and Hooper Cline telling the Judge about the eagle painting.

"And you think this might have been done by the British spy you were telling me about?" The Judge asked Cline.

"I don't know. That's the family tradition."

"Come on, we'll show you the rest of the house," Ham said.

So they showed Judge McGruder everything: the secret room by the fireplace; the room with the fresco of the young man with the pack on his back; the kitchen; the "torture chamber" with its hat rack-umbrella stand; the stairway and the spectacular waterfall; the upstairs bedrooms; the box of old toys;

the dusty furniture stacked in the lean-to at the back.

Hooper Cline offered some information, but the vandals did most of the talking. They presented the house proudly, as if they owned it. Even the old newspapers on the hall walls seemed like minor treasures, because they had been hidden for so long.

After the tour, Hooper Cline and the boys got some chairs from the lean-to, wiped them with a rag and put them in a circle in the "eagle room." They met there like a war council making plans near a battle-field.

First the Judge told Cline about what he had learned from the city planning commission, and about their encounter with Mrs. Frothingham.

"I think there's a chance Treason House can be saved," Judge McGruder concluded. "But it's not going to be easy. Now that I've seen it I'm willing to give it a try. How do the rest of you feel?"

"I worked my fingers to the *bone* on those walls," Marie said. "I don't want some machine crunching the place up after all that."

"Right," Ham agreed. "Did you know I found the eagle that's over the front door? After all we did here, we should have something to say about what happens to the house."

"Besides, it's special." Isabelle looked around the room, lighted now by shafts of late afternoon sunlight. "I've never seen anything like it."

"It reminds me of something I saw on TV once," Dave said. "They had two hundred years of Ameri-

can history in two minutes. A lot of pictures flashed on the screen one after the other, and you weren't quite sure what was happening but it was all there, some way. Treason House is like that. Or like one of those time capsules they bury in buildings, that say 'Open in five hundred years . . .' "

Hooper Cline listened quietly, watching their faces. His usual gloomy expression did not change. "People don't care about that sort of thing now," he said. "There's no chance of saving the house."

"You don't want it to be torn down, do you?" Marie asked him.

"Of course not. It's my home—even though I don't live in it. My mother's family, the Hoopers, owned it for generations."

"Then why not see what can be done to save it?" Carleton McGruder asked him. "With the backing of the County Historical Society, I think we could convince the airport planners to spare the house. So we need a written history, documentary evidence of its age, and an inspection by a committee from the Society. Mr. Cline, could you write the history?"

The old man shook his head. "I'm blind in one eye, and the other one isn't good. I can only read for a few minutes at a time. It would take research, checking facts and dates, going through the old journals . . ."

Marie stood up and pointed at Dave. "He could do it!" she said excitedly. "He's always poking around the library, looking up things in old books. You could tell him what you know about the house, Mr. Cline,

99

and show him where to check."

"Oh, they wouldn't believe a history written by an eleven-year-old kid," Dave said.

"You don't have to put your age on it," Marie insisted. "You always get straight A's in school, and your father works at the newspaper. He can help you. It doesn't have to be a whole book or anything, does it, Judge?"

"I don't see why," Judge McGruder said. "We want something short enough to be read quickly by the committee. Mr. Cline, would you be willing to help David with that?"

Hooper Cline hesitated, then nodded silently.

"Good. I'll go through the deeds and records at the Court House to see if I can't find this documentary evidence Mrs. Frothingham was talking about. There ought to be something there—bills of sale, tax records, contracts—to prove the age of the house."

"What about the rest of us?" Isabelle asked. "What should we do?"

"We could paint the shutters," Marie said. "That's what we were going to do today, before we found out about the house being torn down. Maybe we can nail the broken ones back together, too. If the Historical Society is going to inspect Treason House, we ought to make it look as good as we can. Too bad we can't put new glass in all those broken windows."

"Do you have any idea what that would cost?" Mr. Cline asked sternly. "If I had that sort of money . . ."

Marie decided it would be better to get the conversation off the uncomfortable subject of vandalism and its results. "What about all that old furniture in the back?" she asked. "The rooms seem so empty. Could we clean up some of that and put it around?"

"I don't know what sort of shape it's in," Cline said. "I haven't looked at most of it since I was a young man. My lawyer moved it all to the lean-to when he locked up the house for good. Maybe we could look through it. Some of those pieces are very old, I'm sure."

"Antique furniture would help, when they come to inspect," Judge McGruder said.

Ham looked at his watch. "It's almost four," he said. "We're not going to have time to do all this stuff today."

"Let's go through the furniture today," Marie said, "and then . . . Well, I can come out Monday, I think. How about you, Izzy?"

"I guess so. I don't think I have to babysit Monday."

"Ham?"

"Yeah."

"Dave, you'd better go ahead and work on that history. The rest of us will fix up the house for the inspection . . . if it's all right with you. Mr. Cline." Marie remembered suddenly that she had no business making all these plans without the owner's consent.

Hooper Cline scowled, not in an angry way but as if he were thinking hard. He reached into his pocket, drew out a key ring, and unfastened a silver key which he handed to Marie. "I'd like to know when

101

you're here and what you're doing," he said. "And please give it back when this is all over. That is," he added, "if the house is still standing. Which I doubt."

The cool metal of the key felt peculiar in Marie's hand. She didn't even have a key to her own house.

After an awkward silence, Judge McGruder announced that he had to be getting home and that he'd be in touch with them later in the week. Hooper Cline walked back through the trees to the small house where he lived, and got a cardboard carton which he gave to David. It contained old journals, letters and papers from the Hooper family's past. Dave put it carefully in his basket and left for home. The others went to look through the furniture.

Some of the pieces were broken, and some were not old enough to be especially valuable, but they found a few things to put in each room. There was a tall chest of drawers with rope-like carvings along each side and a sort of pinwheel design across the top; that would look impressive in one of the bedrooms. For the kitchen they found a heavy, round oak table. Chairs with ball-and-claw feet would go in the "eagle room" and there was an odd-shaped sofa with a high back at one end and no back at all at the other end.

"That should go in the torture chamber," Ham said. "Looks more uncomfortable than those benches in the school lunchroom."

It was suppertime before they'd looked at half the things in the lean-to.

Marie, Ham and Izzy came back on Monday, and for at least a few hours every day that week. They dusted and polished the best of the old furniture. Mr. Cline told them where he remembered the things had been in the old days, and they tried to put each piece back in its original place. Dave and his father came out on Wednesday to help move the heaviest pieces.

They found two "oriental" rugs rolled up in the lean-to. The girls vacuumed them with Mr. Cline's vacuum cleaner, scrubbed them with rug shampoo and dried them in the sun. They put one in the hall and one in the eagle room.

There were old pictures hidden behind the stacks

of furniture. A portrait of Lemuel Hooper was their most exciting find. It looked to Marie like the same picture that had been reproduced in the history book Dave had showed her at the library. They hung it in the hallway, just inside the front door. A sampler Mr. Cline thought had been worked by his great-aunt was hung in the bedroom where they'd found the box of toys. It said: "Train up a child in the way he should go, and when he is old he will not depart therefrom."

While the girls worked inside, Ham painted the shutters and fixed them as well as he could. Hooper Cline helped him take them down and replace them when the paint was dry.

Dave spent most of the week working on his history. He told them that his father was helping him by looking through old newspapers on microfilm for possible references to Treason House or the Hooper family. And Judge McGruder had called Dave to give him several dates which had turned up in old records at the Court House.

By Saturday David had finished the first draft of his history. The six of them met that morning at Treason House.

"I wouldn't know the place," Judge McGruder said when Marie led him through the hall to the eagle room. "Rugs, furniture, pictures on the wall— you've done quite a job this week."

They sat in circled chairs again, and Dave opened his notebook and began to read.

10

The History of Treason House
by David A. Keller

Fish built the Hooper house: cod, scrod, swordfish, ocean perch, flounder, haddock, mackerel. They were caught in Prudent Hooper's nets off the coast of New Glasgow and sold to feed the hungry settlers there.

Prudent Hooper was born in Falmouth, England, in 1747. He came to the New World some time before the Revolution because he wasn't doing so well in England. After he piled up the family boat three times off Lizard Point, his father bought him a ticket to New Glasgow.

105

There weren't so many rocks in the harbor here, and everybody liked fish. Prudent Hooper bought his own fishing boat. Then he bought more boats and hired other men to work for him.

The first dated record of this man was his marriage certificate. It said that he married Rachel Mac-Querrie on October 4, 1772. Soon after that he must have started building the house, probably in 1774 or

1775. One of his daughters, Alicia, wrote this in her diary several years later:

> Papa says he wanted to put something called 'wallpaper' in our house when he had it built. But Mother had heard that this 'wallpaper' was poisonous. So instead of that he hired Max Hammerstrom to decorate the house, and that's when all our troubles began . . .

Max Hammerstrom is the Mystery Man in the story of the Hooper house. It seems he came through New Glasgow looking for work as a painter of portraits, tavern signs, or just about anything else. Nobody knew him, and he talked with a foreign accent —but then lots of people did in those days. Prudent Hooper hired him to decorate the walls of the new house he'd built for his bride.

All of this must have happened just before or during the Revolution. The *History of New Glasgow County* says that New Glasgow at that time was especially strong for Independence. The town had been settled by some Scottish families who weren't too fond of the British anyway. Other East Coast towns had many more Tories than New Glasgow. It was only a few men with quite a bit of money who were suspected of having British sympathies—like Prudent Hooper, who was building a large new house.

The *History* says that on the night of March 14, 1777, "an itinerant artist" was seen talking with a British officer in the woods near New Glasgow. He was followed to "a house near Brenner's mill," where a large crowd gathered. "The spy escaped only by taking his own life," it says.

Brenner's Mill was on Rocky Creek (now also known as Cyanide Creek because of the stuff our factories dump into it!), just a few blocks from where the Hooper house still stands. A story passed down through the Hooper family says that Max Hammerstrom was accused of being a spy and jumped to his death from the roof of the new house. So I believe that this house is the one mentioned in the *History of New Glasgow County*, that it was always called Treason House after that night, and that this proves the house is old enough to be saved by the Historical Society.

Was Max Hammerstrom really a spy? Prudent Hooper always maintained that Hammerstrom was innocent. But then I guess he didn't want to admit he'd been fooled. He must have been stubborn about it, because for years after that his neighbors seem to have suspected him of being in on the "treason" too. I don't think he was too popular in New Glasgow after that.

But the Hoopers went on selling fish. They also had nine children. When the five sons got old enough to go into the business, they built bigger ships and started trading voyages all over the world. Three of the daughters got married and settled down. And then there was Alicia.

We know more about Alicia Hooper because she kept a diary. One page of her diary says:

I'm fifteen years old in this Year of Our Lord 1800. Papa says when I'm seventeen I'll marry Melvin Lemon and spend the rest of my life in New Glasgow. I'd jump off the roof like M.H. before I would marry Melvin Lemon!

Alicia was in trouble a lot, and she wrote it all down. Once her brother, a sea captain, brought back a shrunken head from Borneo. She took it to church and sneaked it onto a window ledge during a long prayer. She claimed three women fainted when they saw it. Another time she spent a night in a tree when she was mad about something, and the whole town was looking for her.

That time they called the minister over to talk to her.

"I looked him in the eye and quoted from St. Paul," she wrote later. " 'The good that I would, I cannot do; but I do the very thing I hate.' He didn't seem to know what to say to that."

When she was seventeen Alicia put the diary away and ran off with a boy who was going to make his fortune in the West. Somebody added a note at the front of the diary: "Alicia Jane Hooper, born April 4, 1785, lost in a storm on the Mississippi River in the spring of 1802."

Prudent Hooper died in 1805. His oldest son, Roger, moved into what was now known to everyone as Treason House. Roger had only one son, Lemuel, born in 1815.

Lemuel Hooper carried on the family tradition of being considered an oddball in New Glasgow. He also kept a diary. Most of it is about the religion Lemuel started.

Lemuel's followers called themselves the Nahumites. They based their faith on the book of Nahum in the Bible. From 1836 to 1847, when Lemuel Hooper died, a couple of dozen Nahumites lived in and around Treason House. It's hard to follow the stuff in Lemuel's diary, but it seems the Nahumites believed God spoke only during storms. They would go out and stand on a hill singing and praying in the middle of a summer rain, so it's easy to see why they were considered strange. One page of Lemuel's diary says:

"I am the shatterer. The wrath of God speaks through me. Today I caused the wicked images on the walls of my house to be covered over. Desolation and ruin to Ninevah!"

So it must have been Lemuel who had Max Hammerstrom's frescoes papered over. He was also against slavery. All the Nahumites were strong abolitionists, and there is a tradition that at this time Treason House was a station on the Underground Railroad. Runaway slaves were probably hidden in the "secret room" or "whispering room" beside the fireplace in the main front parlor.

Lemuel Hooper married one of his followers, and they had a son, Samuel, before Lemuel died of pneumonia at the age of 32.

By this time the money the Hoopers had made selling fish and trading all over the world was about gone. Lemuel had been too busy with his religion to work much, and by the time Samuel grew up he and his mother were being supported by some distant cousin. Four of Samuel's unpaid bills were saved by the family and are in the box of documents presented with this history.

Before he could do much about the family fortune, Samuel went off to the Civil War. He wasn't interested in Nahumism and went back to the Presbyterian Church, but he did share his father's abolitionist beliefs. He fought at Gettysburg, and in many other battles. His war record is also enclosed. It says he was wounded in The Wilderness.

After the war, Samuel Hooper married Lucy Peters and went to work in a dry goods store. He did well enough to buy the business, finally. But every once in awhile Samuel had a "spell" when he got to thinking about the war. Sometimes he would go into a kind of trance and wander back to where some of those old battles were fought. He'd be gone for months, and his wife would have to run the store. They had two daughters, Gertrude Hooper and Elizabeth Hooper Cline.

After Samuel and his wife died, Gertrude lived alone in Treason House. She got a man to manage the store. She must have been shy, because she stayed alone most of the time and wrote poetry and stuff. This poem is dated 1902:

Corners of my house,
Webbed and dark with dust,
Hide me.
Rooms of my heart,
Vacant these many years,
Corner me.

"My sister's poetry was never published; it was too gloomy," Elizabeth wrote later. I'll go along with that.

A grocery boy found Gertrude Hooper dead one morning in 1905. Soon after that, Elizabeth Hooper Cline, her husband, George Cline, and their son, Hooper Cline, moved in.

Mrs. Cline wrote down some of the stories she'd heard from her family about Treason House. Her notes are also in the box, and I got some of my facts from them.

Hooper Cline had a brother and a sister, but they both died as children. He was born in 1898, and in 1918 he joined the Army. He didn't see Treason House again for fifty years.

Mr. Cline spent most of that time in the Army. While he was in Europe just after World War I, his father died and his mother started renting rooms to people. When she died, too, a family lawyer rented the whole house to a man named Reginald Galusha.

Reginald Galusha was a phrenologist. The dictionary says phrenology is "the practice of studying character and mental capacity from the conformation of the skull." In other words, it's something like telling fortunes by feeling the bumps on people's heads.

Judge McGruder found out quite a bit about Galusha by looking up his police record. His real name was Jim Larson and he grew up in Brooklyn. Before he came to New Glasgow he'd been arrested four times on "bunco" charges (swindling). There were a couple of complaints while he lived in Treason House, but he must have done a good business there. Mr. Cline says he paid the rent every month.

Hooper Cline didn't know Galusha was a crook, of course. He was still travelling all over the world with the Army. Finally, the police made Galusha leave town some time in the 1930's, and the family lawyer locked up Treason House for good. By that time it was in no condition to rent to anybody.

Hooper Cline fought in Africa, Italy and France in World War II. Even after he retired from the Army he stayed on in Europe for awhile. He'd been there so long it seemed more like home than Connecticut.

When he finally did come back to America in 1955, he walked through Treason House once and locked it up again. It was wired for electricity but had no running water, no heat except a coal stove that didn't work, and those old fireplaces. He didn't have the money to make all the repairs it would need, so he moved into the small house next door which his family had also owned since the days of Lemuel

Hooper. That house had been modernized by his aunt and uncle in the 1920's.

That is the story of Treason House. Maybe it doesn't look like much now. The first time I saw it I thought it was just a broken-down house nobody wanted. But now that I know about it, about how old it is and all the people who lived here, I think it's more important than a few yards of asphalt in an airport parking lot.

I figure that since it was built by Prudent Hooper, Treason House has stood through six wars, a bunch of financial panics and a depression, hundreds of hurricanes, four big fires in New Glasgow, seven floods, two riots and forty years of vandalism. It seems to me the place has earned the right to stay here.

The End

"Dave, that's really neat," Marie said with new respect. "How'd you find out all that?"

"Most of it came from the letters and journals, or from Mr. Cline. I just put it all together." David riffled the pages nervously. "I don't know; it doesn't sound quite like the histories in the library. I tried, but I did it in such a hurry . . ."

"You did a fine job, David," said Judge McGruder.

"You sure did," Izzy agreed. "The part about Alicia was sad, though. 'Lost in a storm on the Mississippi River.' Did she drown?"

"Nobody knows for sure," David told her. "Alicia just sort of disappeared in this terrible storm, and nobody ever heard from her again so they assumed she fell in the river and drowned."

"Bet she didn't," Marie said. "From the sound of that diary, Alicia was too cool to go falling in a river. She probably just got fed up and went off someplace."

"The more I found out about this house, the more mysteries there were," David said. "Like what happened to Alicia? Was Hammerstrom really a spy, and did Prudent Hooper know it? Was Lemuel serious about this Nahumite business or was it just a put-on to hide his work for the Underground Railroad?"

"Tune in tomorrow, for the exciting conclusion to the story of Treason House," Ham added. "I liked the stuff about Galusha—better known as Jim Larson. Was he a crook, Judge?"

"Who can say? A lot of people believed in him. That's the way history is, even recent history. There are always more questions than answers."

Throughout the reading of David's history and the discussion afterwards, Hooper Cline sat quietly, listening. Finally he turned to David and said simply, "Thank you. I didn't think anyone else would ever care about this house again."

"Judge," Ham asked, "can we call the Historical Society now? The history's ready, and the house is almost fixed up. We only have a few more things to do."

"Yes," said the Judge, "I think we're ready to face Mrs. Frothingham again. May we telephone from your house, Mr. Cline?"

They went outside, across the yard that was now neatly trimmed, through the weedy gully and along a path to the much smaller house in which Hooper Cline now lived. It was more a cottage than a house. There was only one floor, topped by a steep-sloped roof. It was the same silver-gray color as Treason House, but its windows were modern and unbroken. Inside there was one large sitting room on the left with a bed made up in one corner, and a kitchen area to the right.

The telephone was bolted to the kitchen wall. While Judge McGruder made his call, the others sat down in the other room and looked around. The furniture was shabby, but clean. On the walls hung a number of portraits in heavy frames, and some photographs of men in Army uniforms.

In a few moments the Judge joined them, looking more than a little annoyed. "Mrs. Frothingham informs me that the committee couldn't possibly schedule an inspection of Treason House for at least six months," he said.

II

"Six months!" Izzy exclaimed.

"Tell 'em to forget it," Ham said. "Unless they want to tour the historical asphalt of the new parking lot."

"Now, don't give up so easily," Judge McGruder told them. "I used to be on the board of directors of the Historical Society. I know most of the members, and just between you and me, Mrs. Frothingham isn't the most popular person. In fact, she gives the others a headache now and then."

"I can believe *that*," Marie muttered.

"Let me check with some other people from the

Historical Society," the Judge went on. "I'll call you in a day or two and let you know what we've worked out."

Both Hooper Cline and David heard from Judge McGruder on Monday afternoon. He told them that a committee from the New Glasgow County Historical Society would tour Treason House at 10:00 a.m. on Saturday, August 5.

"That's less than two weeks from now!" Marie said when Dave called to tell her the news. "The sofa needs stuffing, and Ham isn't done with those shutters . . ."

"We'll just have to do as much as we can by then."

"What'd they say about your history?"

"Nothing, yet. Judge McGruder's having copies typed and sent to each member of the inspection committee, so they can read it before they come. There's four of them."

"Dear Mrs. Frothingham is one, of course?"

"Naturally."

"Nuts! She'll hate it no matter what."

"At least we've got a chance, Bellotti."

Marie got up early on the Saturday morning of the inspection. She ironed the navy blue dress she usually wore to church and put it on. The four vandals had agreed to dress up for the occasion, so that they would make the best possible impression on the committee.

With her hair tied in two sleek pigtails and her best shoes shined to a gleaming black, Marie decided she looked innocent enough even for Mrs. Frothingham. "Little goody two-shoes," she sneered at her image in the mirror.

She met Izzy outside, and the two of them rode out to Treason House. Marie felt silly, pedaling along in her best clothes, carefully avoiding puddles and dusty stretches.

Halfway to Orchard Road they passed a house that was being wrecked. A few months ago, Marie would not have given it a second glance. Buildings were always being torn down in New Glasgow. Now she stared at the old house that was rapidly becoming a pile of rubble. She saw the pitiful shreds of paper and paint that someone had once used to brighten the place. She watched the huge wrecking machines surround the remains of the house like bullies circling a victim they'd already knocked to the ground.

"Oh, don't be stupid," Marie told herself angrily. "It's just an old dump . . ."

"What?" Isabelle asked her.

"Nothing. I was just thinking, that's what they'll be doing to Treason House in a few weeks."

"If we don't convince the committee to save it, you mean."

"Yeah. If."

Ham and David were there when the girls arrived. Dave had combed his hair back somehow so it didn't look so long, and he wore a clean, dark shirt and new-looking pants. Ham twitched uncomfortably in a similar outfit. Even Mr. Cline had prepared for the occasion by putting on a suit, white shirt and tie.

They stood awkwardly in the hall until they heard

119

a car stop in front of the house. Then they watched on the front porch while the committee, accompanied by Judge McGruder, got out of a huge black Continental.

Mrs. Frothingham looked bored and superior as the Judge introduced the rest of the committee. There was a small, incredibly thin woman named Mrs. Ruether, who taught history at the University. She smiled encouragingly as the introductions went on. The two men, Mr. Wadsworth and Mr. Long, seemed stiff and formal but not really frightening. Looking the group over, Marie began to hope a little.

"You'll want to see the outside of the house before you go in," Judge McGruder told them. "As you read in the history, it was built in 1774 or 1775 . . ."

"According to family tradition," Mrs. Frothingham put in sharply. "I must say, Carleton, that so-called history was rather short on documentary proof. And as for that wild story about a spy leaping off the widow's walk . . ."

"I enjoyed the history," said Mr. Wadsworth. "At least it was a lot more interesting than some I've had to plow through. Shorter, too. But we do have to ask: is there any proof that the house dates back to colonial times?"

"We couldn't come up with any legal records," the Judge admitted. "As you know, documents like that from the eighteenth century are rather rare. But I did find records of taxes being paid on the house very soon after Independence. David has a box of things he'll show you later that include some references to the Hooper House from the 1790's."

"Look at the carving on that wooden rail along the roof," said Mr. Long. "It's certainly the Georgian style."

"You know very well Georgian architecture went on even into the nineteenth century," Mrs. Frothingham told him. "That's no proof."

Long glared at her, and Marie had to bite her lips to keep from smiling.

"What an interesting eagle over the door," Mrs. Reuther said, stepping closer to peer at it. "I believe it's hand carved, but there's something odd about it. The eagle was a common symbol, of course, but I've never seen one quite like this."

"I found it in the secret room," Ham volunteered. "It's like the picture over the fireplace . . ."

"Well, we may as well go in," Mrs. Frothingham interrupted as though Ham did not even exist.

In the dim light of the hallway, Marie thought the charm of Treason House must surely come through, even to the critical Mrs. Frothingham. Marie and Izzy had polished the woodwork around the doors until it shone. The soft, faded colors of the oriental rug swam across the floor like dim fish-shapes in a pool. And the stairway, with its curving banister and waterfall fresco, seemed almost to flow down from the second story to meet them.

Mrs. Reuther moved to study the fresco, running her fingers over it lightly. "Beautiful," she said. "Possibly someone at the University could test a bit of this paint and tell us how old it is."

"You know how long that takes, Lucille," said Mrs. Frothingham. "Besides, it's summer. The laboratories aren't likely to be operating now." She pronounced the word "la-*bor*-a-tories."

"It's quite well-preserved, if it is two hundred years old," Mr. Wadsworth said. "What are these bits of paper sticking to the fresco in spots?"

"Wallpaper," David told him. "We just found the fresco a few weeks ago, when we were peeling off the old paper that had covered it for years and years. Some professional could do a better job of cleaning it up, but we didn't want to hurt the picture."

"I believe Judge McGruder required these children to work here as part of a court probation, after they were caught vandalizing the property," Mrs. Frothingham explained viciously.

Hooper Cline turned his back on her and walked to the door of the eagle room. "This was the formal sitting room in the old days," he said. "I think you'll want to look at the painting over the fireplace."

"Another eagle," Mrs. Reuther commented. "My, what a handsome bird. The Hoopers must have been a patriotic family. You know, I think that's what interests me most about these old houses. When a man builds a house, he makes a sort of statement about himself and his times. You can tell a great deal about people by looking at their homes."

"From the unusual aspects of this house, and some of the stories in that history the young man wrote," said Mr. Long, "I believe this family was quite a colorful one. No offense, Mr. Cline."

Cline's mouth stretched into his peculiar smile. "Colorful, yes. The Hoopers were always a bit out of step, it seems. They went their own way."

Marie thought about that as they walked through the rest of Treason House with the committee. The story of the Hoopers fascinated her, and had a lot to do with her feeling that their house must not be destroyed. She liked them because they'd never been afraid to be different.

When the group got upstairs, Mrs. Frothingham pointed out that none of the toys Izzy had dusted and displayed were more than a hundred years old. Mr. Long exclaimed over the beauty of the carving on a wooden chest of drawers, but Mr. Cline had to admit that he had no idea who had made the chest or when. That was the way it went.

Even the secret room did not impress them as much as Marie had hoped. It seemed that many old houses had spaces like it beside the main fireplace, and there was no way to prove that it had ever been used to hide runaway slaves.

"I'm impressed with the amount of work you four youngsters have done here," Mr. Wadsworth said kindly as they looked at the fresco of the young man with the pack on his back.

Judge McGruder glared at Mrs. Frothingham. "I want you all to know," he said, "that they were legally discharged almost a month ago. Everything they've done since then has been voluntary."

Finally the tour was finished, and the committee met in the eagle room while the others waited in the

124

kitchen.

"They're not gonna do anything," Ham said. He took a stick of gum out of his pocket and crammed it into his mouth.

Izzy had not given up yet. "I think the others liked the house. It was just that one woman . . ."

"Old lady Frothingham will think up plenty of reasons to get the others on her side," Marie said. "It's my fault. Ever since I broke her precious model that day, I've been poison."

"One person won't make the decision," Judge Mc-Gruder assured them. "If anything, the other three would like to go against Millicent. If only we had some kind of documentary evidence to show when the house was built. That's the real problem."

Mr. Cline leaned against the wall, looking very old all at once. "I've gone through all my family papers, boxes in the attic, everything. But I was away so long, you see. I just don't know where I could find proof like that."

"When is the construction company due to start here, Mr. Cline?" asked the Judge.

"August 17."

It was less than two weeks away.

"We're ready to speak to you now," Mr. Long said from the hall doorway. After one look at his face, Marie was sure the answer would be no.

"All of us feel that this house is a treasure and certainly deserves to be restored and maintained," Long began when they were all in the eagle room. "Unfortunately, the funds of the New Glasgow

County Historical Society are very limited. We are already responsible for the upkeep of a number of old houses in this area, and our budget runs considerably in the red every year."

"For the time being," Mr. Wadsworth added, "we've had to limit new properties to those of the colonial era. And there just isn't any conclusive proof that this house is that old."

"You understand that I would be willing to give the house to the Society," said Mr. Cline. "I'd rather do that than see it destroyed."

"That's very generous," Mr. Long told him. "But you see, so many repairs would have to be made just to keep the house from falling into complete ruin."

Mrs. Frothingham could not stay out of the discussion any longer. "This house, and others like it, have been victimized by vandals for years. All those broken windows, the cracks and holes in the plaster, the cuts and scratches in the woodwork: it would take a great deal of money, indeed, to get this building ready for display." She looked significantly at the four vandals.

"But if you could just persuade the builders of the new airport to leave the house, we might finance restoration later," Judge McGruder suggested. "All we're asking you now is to tell them the place should be spared."

Mrs. Reuther shook her head, looking genuinely sorry. "You know, Judge, that they wouldn't agree unless we could give them some reason other than the fact that the house is old and interesting. They would want to know what's going to be done with it, what value it has now."

"There are foundations, Federal funds, private organizations," the Judge insisted. "Surely we could find money somewhere. The problem now is time. The wreckers will be here in two weeks."

"Carleton," Mrs. Frothingham said with a self-satisfied smile, "we all appreciate your interest in this house, and in these young—people. I'm sure we can find room for some of the better furniture in our museum. And I will personally see to it that a photographer comes before the, er, removal of the house, to make a complete record . . ."

"Pictures!" Marie snorted. She'd meant to keep still, but Mrs. Frothingham was just too much. "You can't keep this house in pictures. It's a *place*, and when it's gone it'll be gone forever."

"If there were anything we could do," Mrs. Reuther said helplessly, "I'm sure we'd be happy to . . ."

"I expected you'd say what you did." Mr. Cline's voice was hard, and he looked closed and angry like he had the first time they'd seen him. "Thank you for coming."

He led the way to the door. The committee members walked across the yard with the Judge, who turned once to look back regretfully.

Ham reached up, ripped the wooden eagle from its place over the door, and hurled it into the weeds on the far side of the house.

12

The black Continental roared off on the road toward downtown New Glasgow, and in the dust behind it Ham pedaled furiously away from Treason
House without a backward glance. At the same time,
Hooper Cline grunted some sort of goodbye and
limped off to his house.

"I've got to go, too," Izzy said. "My mother's due
at work in a little while; she's filling in for someone
who's sick and I have to babysit. Maybe I can catch
up with Arnold on the way and talk to him. He's *so*
touchy!"

Marie took the silver key out of her dress pocket
and had put in in the lock before she realized what

she was doing. "Hey, this is dumb," she said. "Might as well let everybody rip the place to pieces. It'll be gone soon enough anyway." But she turned the key before she replaced it in her pocket. "I guess I should take this back to Mr. Cline before I go home."

David had walked over to the weeds and picked up the carved wooden eagle. "This could be saved, anyway," he said, studying it thoughtfully. Then he stopped in his tracks. "Of course! That's it! Why didn't I think of it before?"

"What are you talking about?"

"The eagle! I know what's strange about it, and the one over the fireplace, too. They're backwards!"

"Backwards?"

"Reversed. You know the eagles you see in patriotic drawings, or on the Great Seal of the United States—they always face right, toward their own right shoulders. This one has its head turned to the left. And another thing, it's black. I'm sure that isn't just age stains. Did you ever see a black eagle?"

"I don't know. I never thought about it."

"These aren't American eagles, Bellotti," David said, his voice rising with excitement.

"What do you mean? What are they, then?"

"I don't know. But I'm going to find out. Come on, you can help."

Dave laid the eagle beside the door and jumped on his bike without even telling her where they were going. She followed, mystified, but glad to have something to think about besides their dismal failure with the committee from the New Glasgow County Historical Society. They left their bicycles in the rack in front of the library and hurried into the big research room.

"What are we looking for?" Marie whispered.

"That eagle, of course! Here, you look through this pictorial history of the Revolution. I'm going to hunt up a book on 18th century heraldry."

It took most of the afternoon, but David finally found what he was looking for. He dropped a heavy book triumphantly onto the table in front of Marie and pointed to a picture at the top of a page.

And there it was. The Treason House eagle, black, its huge wings spread, its head turned to the left. The caption said:

> *Prussian Eagle.* Symbol of Imperial Prussia. Brought to the United States by immigrants and especially by the 17,000 'Hessian' soldiers who fought with the British during the Revolutionary War. These Prussian mercenaries took part in almost every battle of the war and many stayed to become permanent citizens of the new nation.

"I don't get it," Marie said. "You think the Hoopers were really Hessians or Prussians or whatever you call it?"

"No, no, Max Hammerstrom, the spy! Remember, those old diaries said he talked with a foreign accent. What if he was really a Hessian, hired by the British to spy for them? I'm sure I read someplace that a lot of New England homes were decorated by wandering artists during and after the war. What if that eagle were some kind of signal to his contacts?"

130

"I don't know," Marie said doubtfully. "It sounds like a lot of 'what if's' to me. Anyway, what difference does it make now? The house is doomed."

"Don't you see? If we could prove the spy story was true, that would prove that the house was already there during the Revolutionary War. Then it would qualify to be saved and restored."

"You don't give up very easy, do you?" Marie looked at Dave with a new respect. He was a bookworm, but he had guts. "What do we do now?" she asked.

"I'm going to call that Mrs. Reuther, the woman from the committee who teaches history at the University. I want to see what she thinks about this. Maybe she'll let me check in the University library, too."

"She seemed to really like the house," Marie said. "It won't hurt to call her. What do you want me to do?"

"Get hold of Izzy and Ham. Tell 'em what we found out, and see if they can go back to the house with us after supper tonight. I want to go over that whole place one more time. We looked at those eagles all this time without figuring what they were. Maybe there's something else we missed."

Marie went home, changed clothes, and fixed herself a cold chicken sandwich. It was a relief to relax in a sweatshirt and jeans after being dressed up for most of the day. She told her mother briefly about their session with the Historical Society committee. Mrs. Bellotti said she was sorry, but she looked rather pleased that the whole affair was finally over. She'd never seen Treason House.

Tonight the Bellottis were going to Mr. and Mrs. Costa's for a card party, so there was no need for Marie to mention her plan to go back to the house after supper, as long as she was home early.

After her mother left for the beauty shop, Marie called Isabelle. "Dave thinks he's found something new," she said. "He's figured out something about that eagle—we'll explain it to you later. Anyway, can you come out to the house about seven tonight?"

"I guess so. I was going to wash my hair, but . . ."

"Do it tomorrow. Think of all that work we did! It's not going to be for nothing, if I can help it. Did you talk to Ham?"

"Yes, I tried. I rode part of the way home with him. He didn't say much; he's just mad at the world right now."

"I'll call him. See you at seven."

Ham's older brother Will answered the telephone. Marie heard his teasing voice: "Oh Arnold! There's a *girl* calling you! Come on, baby brother, your girl-friend's waiting." Then all through the conversation she could hear laughing and scuffling in the background, so she knew Will was still there, and probably some of his friends too.

"We're going back to the house tonight," she told Ham. "Dave wants to look all through it one more time, for some kind of evidence of when it was built."

"What's the use?" Ham growled. "I'm sick of that old place. Let 'em wreck it, I don't care."

132

"You know that wooden eagle? Dave found a picture of it in a history book. It's a Prussian eagle, not American. Dave says maybe that spy was a Prussian, working for the British. Maybe there's something we missed on one of the frescoes, a date or a signature or something. Can you come?"

"It won't do any good."

"Come on, just one more try."

"I guess."

The background noise grew louder, and Ham hung up suddenly. Marie could understand his surly disposition when she thought what it must be like to live with an older brother like Will Schmidt.

Marie volunteered to do the dishes while her mother got ready to go to the card party. Still, it was nearly seven when the Bellottis left. Marie told them casually that she might go out for awhile with her friends. She had a strong feeling that her mother would not approve of another trip to Treason House now that the committee had made its decision, so she did not mention their destination.

She wiped the dishes hastily and crammed them into the cupboard. Izzy was waiting on the steps when she went out the door.

Ham and Dave arrived at the house ahead of them. The boys were tossing a Frisbee in the yard when Marie and Isabelle got there. The shadows of the long summer twilight were just beginning to creep out in front of Treason House.

"Mrs. Reuther was great!" Dave told them. "She said she thought I was right about the eagle. She met me at the University library and helped me look up some stuff about Hessian soldiers and spies in the Revolution, and we actually found a reference to Max Hammerstrom!"

"That should prove it, then," said Isabelle.

"Not quite. His name was in a secret list of men on the payroll of the British army, one that just turned up a few years ago. The historians assume that they were spies. But there's no mention of Treason House, nothing to tie him with the Hoopers."

"At least it shows there was a Max Hammerstrom, and he was working for the redcoats," Marie said.

"Yeah, that's something." Dave put the Frisbee in his bike basket and took out a flashlight. "Come on, let's look around before it gets dark. Even now it's going to be sort of murky in there; that's why I brought this."

They started with the frescoes, picking off bits of wallpaper that they could get loose and peering at every mark that might be a signature or a date. Ham went over the secret room again, using Dave's flashlight to examine every corner. Marie searched the lean-to and looked in each drawer in the old furniture. They found nothing.

"Let's try upstairs," Dave said.

"It's getting pretty dark." Izzy looked around at the old house, which seemed to grow bigger as the shadows became thicker.

"We can use the flashlight, and there's some candles up there. Come on." Dave led the way up the curving staircase.

In the "playroom," the girls lit a candle and looked through the toys again. Marie heard a sort of scratching sound in the area of a small chest of drawers in one corner of the room. At first she thought it was a tree branch brushing the shutter outside, but finally she went with her candle to look.

A small, dark shape scuttled across the floor, brushed over her bare toes exposed by the sandals she'd worn, and vanished into the upstairs hall.

Marie didn't exactly scream, but she let out a yelp of surprise.

"What's wrong?" Izzy asked, jumping up.

"Rats! Yech! Well, maybe mice." Marie shuddered, still feeling the tiny paws scampering over her foot.

Behind the small chest they found a nest of baby mice. By this time the boys had come to see what had happened.

"All that screaming over a few little mice?" Ham asked.

"I wasn't screaming," Marie protested. "One of 'em just startled me, ran right over my foot."

"They're sort of cute," Izzy said, bending down to get a closer look.

"Shhh," Dave told them suddenly.

For a moment there was no sound but the ordinary evening noises of the city and the creaking of the old wooden house. Marie had noticed before that Treason House was never really quiet. Its wooden skeleton seemed to shift and settle all the time like an old man's bones.

Then they heard a crunching noise from the gravel of the driveway in front of the house. It was not like the sound of steady footsteps coming up the drive. The noise was soft, and sneaky.

The front door rattled slightly, and clicked shut.

"Bellotti, did you lock the door?" Dave whispered.

"How could I? We're inside, and the padlock's outside."

"Somebody else is inside now, too."

They listened, but it was impossible to sort out the creaking of the house from whatever sounds the intruder might be making. Marie could not stand there anymore, so she tiptoed through the upstairs hall to one of the front bedrooms. The others followed, and they looked through the broken shutter of a window that faced the street.

The street lights were on, though it was not completely dark outside yet. There was no car in view, nothing to show that anyone had come into Treason House.

"Maybe we imagined it," Izzy whispered.

"All four of us?" asked Ham.

"It's probably the ghost of Max Hammerstrom, come back to haunt us so we won't find out his dreadful secret." Marie intended that as a joke, but nobody smiled, and it did not seem funny to her either after she said it.

"Kids break in here all the time, right?" Ham whispered. "So it's probably just a couple of kids. Why don't we go down and scare them away? Man, they'd fly if we came screeching down the stairs all of a sudden."

"Our bikes are outside," Dave reminded him. "And the lock's hanging open. Whoever it is has got to know there's somebody in here."

"Maybe it's Mr. Cline," Izzy said hopefully. "Maybe he saw the lights and came over to check."

"He knows our bikes; he'd have called to us by now," Dave told her.

Marie was scared. The only cure she knew for that was doing something. "Come on," she said. "I'm not going to hide up here all night like a treed cat. It's late; I should be home by now. Let's go."

She tried to walk casually to the stairway, but her feet insisted on tiptoeing. She wished she'd worn her sneakers instead of sandals. Ham tripped over the uneven floor just as they reached the head of the stairs, and that removed any possibility of surprise. Marie started down, telling herself that there was nobody there.

With a sick, queasy feeling, she saw something tall and dark against the wall near the front door. Long arms, reaching out—then she realized it was the umbrella stand, which they'd brought out of the "torture chamber" and placed by the door. The hall was empty.

Marie relaxed, disgusted at her own wild imagination. Then, just as she reached the bottom of the stairs, the door to the room with the eagle painting was hurled open and a deep voice yelled "Arrrrghhh!"

13

Will Schmidt and two of his friends ran into the
hall and stood shrieking with laughter at the success
of their joke. The girls had screamed in terror. All
four of the young vandals had run halfway up the
stairs before they looked back and saw the intruders.

"Will, you rotten creep!" Ham shouted, his face
pink with anger.

"Why, little brother, did we scare you?" Will
smiled unpleasantly.

"What are you doing out here, anyway?"

"We heard that this place is going to be wiped
out," Will said, lighting a cigarette. "Seemed like a
good time to have a little fun. If you tots are good,

we might let you in on a real rip-off."

One of the boys with Will opened a paper sack, took out an over-ripe tomato and hurled it at the wall. It landed on the waterfall with a sodden splat.

"No!" Ham raced down the stairs and stood a few feet from his brother, fists clenched. "We found out some new stuff. They might not tear the place down, after all. Come on, Will, go someplace else!"

"You still think those Historical Society dudes are going to pay attention to you? Man, are you dumb! They don't care if George Washington slept here or whatever old junk you've dug up about this dump. The Wheels downtown say the new airport goes here, and so the new airport goes here. Grow up, kid! That's the way it is."

Ham stood his ground. "Maybe. But we want to try one more time."

The tall boy who had thrown the tomato looked at them curiously. "What's it to you? Is the old guy that owns the place slipping you a few bucks?"

"It's a neat house; we like it," Marie said. "Besides, we worked half the summer getting it cleaned up. Couldn't you go make a mess someplace else?" Marie hated the scared, pleading sound of her voice, but that was the way it came out.

"We want to have our fun right here." The third high school boy spoke with a mean grin. Marie knew him by sight; he was called Leon Alvarez. Sometimes he stopped grade school kids outside the school fence and took their lunch money. She was pretty sure he'd been at Treason House the night of the carnival, when they'd been caught by the police.

Dave must have been thinking the same thing. "You guys were out here before," he said. "We didn't tell on you then, but . . ."

Alvarez pretended to cower behind Will. "Oh, I'm scared," he said. "They're gonna set the fuzz on us!"

Will reached out and grabbed Dave's shirt collar, twisting it in his hand. "Oh, no, they're not," he said. He flipped the butt of his cigarette away and seized Ham in the same way with the other hand. "It's about time you brats learned how to make it in this town. You don't mess around with cops and judges. You have all the fun you want and laugh about it afterwards and don't get caught. And you never, never rat on anybody."

To Marie's astonishment, it was timid Isabelle who ran forward and kicked Will in the shin. "Let them alone," she cried. She took Will by surprise, too. He dropped the boys and rubbed his leg, glaring at her angrily.

Ham moved back out of his brother's reach, but as he went he said: "I won't cover for you this time, Will."

He sounded like he meant it. Marie was proud of him, and of Izzy, and Dave and herself, too. It was nice to be treated well by older kids, like they had been when they'd followed along that first night at Treason House. But it was even better, somehow, to find out you had the guts to stand up to them.

"Look!" Izzy yelled suddenly.

By the door to the eagle room was a pile of oily

rags Dave had been using to clean the painting over the fireplace. Will's cigarette had landed there, smoldered for a moment and then flashed into a blaze that was already catching the woodwork and eating its way along the rug.

"All *right*," cheered Alvarez. "That's better than tomatoes and paint. Too bad we didn't bring marsh-mallows!"

Dave raced over and kicked the rags apart with his feet, trying to stamp out the flames. "Call the fire department!" he yelled.

"But there's no phone!" Marie saw the rug in the eagle room beginning to burn. She'd read somewhere about smothering fires, so she began trying to roll it up. The three high school boys stood watching, their faces excited in the flickering light.

"This joint will go up like a bonfire," Will said. "We better go outside to watch, and be ready to take off if the red wagons do show up. Come on, brats, get out while you can. Where's my little brother?"

Ham was nowhere in sight. For the first time that night, Will Schmidt looked uncertain, even worried.

"He was right here," Marie said helplessly.

"That kid's dumb enough to get caught upstairs," Will said. "Ham! Come on, let's get out of here!"

There was no answer. Dave backed out of the eagle room, coughing and choking, his eyes watering from the smoke. "We can't stop it; we'd better go."

"Arnold isn't here," Izzy told him.

"He probably went outside already," Dave said. *"Ham?"*

Ham still did not answer, so they all stumbled out the front door. Marie's eyes were watering, too, and she was not sure whether it was entirely from the smoke. The house looked almost normal from the yard, except for a faint flickering light behind some of the downstairs shutters.

All those years, she thought. All the people who lived their whole lives here. All the hours we scrubbed and swept and peeled wallpaper. Still, maybe it was better than a wrecking crew. It would be quick, and clean.

"Ham's not out here, either," Will said. "That stupid kid. You don't think he went upstairs?"

Then they saw Ham and Hooper Cline coming along the path from Mr. Cline's house. At almost the same moment, they heard the siren of a fire engine.

"Here they come," said Leon Alvarez. "We better get out of here."

"Why?" Will's assurance was back, now that he knew his brother was not trapped in the burning house. "We did 'em a favor; now they won't have to knock the place down. I'll bet we saved the city a bundle." But he moved away with the others as the siren grew louder. The three of them slipped into the darkness just as the fire engine pulled up in front of Treason House.

Dave, Marie, Ham and Izzy stood with Hooper Cline in the yard as the firemen rushed into the house. Long, black hoses snaked into the house, and the flames protested with a snakelike hiss when water sprayed over them. Clouds of smoke billowed out

143

the front door. And finally Marie realized that she did not see flames behind the shutters any more.

"It's out," Dave said softly.

"Good thing the firemen got here when they did," said Marie. "Was it you who called them, Ham?"

"Mr. Cline. I ran over and told him."

"You were the only one who thought about using his phone," Isabelle said.

"Phone!" Marie croaked, looking suddenly at her watch. "Good grief, it's after nine! Mr. Cline, could I call my folks from your house? They've probably called by now to see if I'm home . . ."

Izzy was equally late, so the girls went together to Mr. Cline's house. Marie called her mother at the Costas' party, trying her best to make the delay sound harmless and unimportant.

"We came out to do a couple of things for Mr. Cline, and Ham Schmidt's brother accidentally started a little, um, fire. No, nobody was hurt, it was just mostly smoke. Yes, it's out. No, it wasn't our fault, Mom, it was an accident. I'll be home in an hour or so. Yes, I'll be careful."

When they got back to Treason House after Izzy's call, Judge McGruder's car was parked near the fire truck. The Judge stood in the yard with the members of the committee from the New Glasgow County Historical Society.

"What are they doing here?" Marie whispered to Dave.

"More of our great luck," Dave told her. "I called Judge McGruder this afternoon and told him what I'd found out, about the eagle and everything. He said he'd try to get the committee to come out here once more, and maybe reconsider—but I didn't think he meant tonight!"

Mrs. Frothingham turned, and she pointed a long finger with a scarlet-painted nail. "There they are," she said in her shrill voice. "You see, I told you youngsters like that couldn't be trusted with the treasures of the past. They simply run wild, do as they please, no discipline . . . "

"Now, Millicent," said the Judge. "We don't even know how the fire started."

"You can't tell me they didn't have something to do with it!"

Marie clamped her mouth shut, wishing she *could* tell the committee they'd had nothing to do with the fire.

"It wasn't our fault . . ." Ham began, and then hesitated.

"You were in the house at the time?" Judge McGruder asked.

"Yes, but we didn't start it." Dave looked at Ham.

At that moment Hooper Cline and one of the firemen came to join the group on the lawn. "We're trying to determine the cause of the fire," the fireman said. "Can you kids tell us anything?"

The four vandals looked at each other. The adults watched them, and waited. Marie wondered whether Judge McGruder could still send them to reform school. Even if they told the truth, it would sound like the same old excuses.

"My brother and his friends started it," Ham said finally.

145

Before they could question him any further, a police car pulled up beside the group. Two policemen got out and led Will Schmidt and his friends to Mr. Cline.

"We saw these kids running away just as the fire truck arrived," one of the policemen said. "You know them?"

"I've never seen them before," said Mr. Cline.

"We know you've had a lot of trouble with vandalism," the other policeman said. "Looks like these three are likely suspects. And if we find evidence of arson, they won't bother you again for a long time."

"Arson!" Will's face went pale, and he shifted nervously from one foot to the other. "We didn't do anything. The fire was an accident! Ham, tell 'em. Hey, you guys, come on . . ." He was almost begging.

"You sure you want us to?" Ham asked his brother.

The older boys nodded eagerly. So Ham told it; everything. He didn't leave out their threat of a "rip-off" in Treason House that night or the fact that Will and his friends had been there without permission from Mr. Cline or anyone else. But when Ham came to the part about the fire, he admitted that it had been an accident.

"I guess it was partly our fault, too," he said. "We shouldn't have left those oily rags in the hall."

"These three made no effort to help you put out the fire, did they?" the first policeman asked.

"No, they didn't," Dave said.

"We knew the joint was going to be torn down

146

anyway," Will protested. "So what's the difference if it goes a few days early?"

"There's still the matter of trespassing on private property," the policeman said. He peered around at the group on the lawn and noticed Judge McGruder for the first time. "Judge, I didn't know you were here. What do you think; shall we take them in?"

"Certainly." Judge McGruder looked stern and tough, as he had the day Marie and the others had appeared before him. "The courts are cracking down on vandals, you know. I think we can teach these boys a lesson."

As the squad car drove away with Will and his friends, the firemen began rolling up their hoses and putting the other equipment away. A few wisps of smoke seeped through the cracks around the windows, but otherwise there was no sign of the condition of the house inside.

"We may as well go home," Mrs. Frothingham said. "Whatever it was you dragged us away from the Van Brocks' party to see, Carleton, there's no point in it now. These delinquents of yours have taken care of this house, once and for all."

The fireman who seemed to be in charge overheard her, and stopped to speak to them. "Actually, there's surprisingly little damage," he said. "Those old rugs smoldered slowly. A couple of pieces of furniture burned, and there's a mess from smoke and water. But the floors and walls don't seem to be hurt. You can go in and look around if you want to." He handed his high-powered flashlight to Hooper Cline.

147

14

They all went into the house together: Hooper Cline, Judge McGruder, Marie, Dave, Izzy and Ham, and the committee from the New Glasgow County Historical Society.

The charred remains of the oriental rug in the hall lay in a huge puddle. Mr. Cline flashed the light along the walls, and in the front half of the hall they were blackened by smoke. The woodwork around the door to the eagle room had burned to an uneven outline. Only the stairway and the waterfall fresco had been untouched by the fire.

In the eagle room, two fine old chairs had been reduced to charcoal. The rug was ruined there, too, and the walls and ceiling were black, the eagle over the fireplace was almost unrecognizable, it was so wet and sooty.

Marie rubbed at her stinging eyes, for the air was still smoky. "This place looks worse than it did when we came out to clean it up the first time!" she said miserably.

"It doesn't really matter," Mr. Cline told her. "As that boy said to the police, it's going to be torn down anyway. A few days can't make much difference."

Even now, Dave was unwilling to leave it at that. He clicked on his own flashlight and shined it on the painting. "I called Judge McGruder today because I just noticed some things about this," he said, looking at the committee members. "For one thing, it's not the usual American eagle. It's black—it was even before the fire—and with those funny-looking wings and feet I think it's a Prussian eagle."

"He's right," Mrs. Reuther said. "I didn't think about it when we were here before, but that's what it is."

"That can't mean much." Mr. Long spoke kindly, but he was obviously not impressed. "You know these old houses had all sorts of different paintings, done by traveling artists. Some of them were Germans or Prussians, of course. The eagle is a little unusual, but . . ."

"There's something else," Dave insisted. "Look, it's facing left. The eagle nearly always faces right when it's used as a symbol. So why is this one reversed?"

"Why?" Judge McGruder asked him.

"I don't know, that is, I'm not sure." Dave hesitated, on uncertain ground now. "But if this house had been built and decorated after the Revolution, I believe it would have had a standard American eagle, not a Prussian eagle facing left. I think this painting has something to do with the tradition that calls this place Treason House, and the story about a spy who did these paintings, and I believe the whole thing proves that the house is old enough to be protected by your committee."

"Nonsense!" Mrs. Frothingham turned to leave. "It's all speculation. There's no proof to any of this. We're wasting our time."

"If it were taken down and cleaned, there might be a name or a date or something," Marie said, walking quickly toward the fireplace to hold the committee's attention for a few more seconds. Her sandals made a squishing sound as she crossed the wet carpet. "Look, all that smoke and water loosened it. I think I can get it down . . ."

She pulled carefully at one corner of the picture. With a sort of ripping sound it peeled away from the backboard above the fireplace and came off in her hands. At the same time, several pieces of paper fluttered to the smoke-blackened mantelpiece.

"What's this?" Ham asked idly, picking up one of the yellow scraps. "Looks like chicken tracks. I can't make it out."

"Let me see." Mrs. Reuther took the paper from him and held it carefully, then got the flashlight from Dave. She studied the paper for what seemed like a long time.

150

"Well?" Marie asked. "What is it?"

"A letter. It's written in some sort of code. I think I could figure it out if I had time to study it. There's a key mentioned, a page from one of Shakespeare's plays . . ."

"That's very interesting, but it's late and I'd like to go home," Mrs. Frothingham said from the doorway. "This code, or whatever it is, doesn't establish the age of the house."

The others, excited about the old letters, ignored her. She looked quite forlorn, suddenly, standing there alone. Marie was almost sorry for her. It must be terrible to have to be right all the time, and to have everyone dislike you so much.

"There is a date on the letter," Mrs. Reuther said. "October 4, 1777."

"That's it!" Dave yelled.

Everyone started talking at once, peering at the coded letter and the painting. "I thought the Revolution was in 1776," Marie whispered to Dave.

"It went on until 1783," he told her. "Besides, this just shows the house was here in 1777. It might have been built even earlier."

Mrs. Frothingham stood at the edge of the chattering group, her mouth drawn down at the corners. "Those letters could have been put there later," she insisted. "It's all guesswork."

Now Mrs. Reuther looked at the other sheets of paper that had been behind the painting, one by one. Three others were in code, and she laid them aside.

"There are two letters here that aren't coded," she said finally. "I'll read them, because I think they'll

152

answer even your objections, Millicent. The first one is dated October 17, 1777, and it's addressed to Max Hammerstrom, Hooper House, New Glasgow."

"Our spy!" Ham said with delight.

Mrs. Reuther read:

> Dear Max: I write this in English for the practice, as we agreed. We miss you and hope your work is going well. Always you were happiest with a brush in your hand. Perhaps when this war is over at last you'll be free to make a career for yourself as a painter. Be careful, Max, and take no needless chances. I am well, only very tired and lonely. It was better when we were together. I delivered your letters to C. C. and will bring his reply when the eagle sinister signals it is safe to come.
>
> Your brother, Konrad

"What's an eagle sinister?" Ham asked.

"Sinister means left," Mr. Long said. "That wooden eagle over the door, the one that's just like this painting, must have been used as some sort of signal. I suppose the British told their couriers to look for an eagle facing left on the house where Hammerstrom was staying. It's beginning to sound like those old stories were true."

"Listen to the other letter," Mrs. Reuther said. "There's no date on this one, but my guess is that Hammerstrom intended to leave it when he moved on or went back to the British army. It's addressed to Lemuel Hooper."

"Instead," said Hooper Cline, "he was caught somehow. A mob surrounded the house, and he jumped off the roof, leaving the letters hidden behind the painting all these years. What does it say?"

Mrs. Reuther read it:

> Sir: I sincerely hope you are pleased with the pictures I leave in your house. I believe them to be the best work I have ever done. I say this so that you will never think I have abused your hospitality, or stayed with you under false pretenses. I am an artist, as I told you. But you did not know that I came to this country as a hired soldier, with a duty to the English king.
>
> My brother and I were forced to leave home because times were bad and my father could not support his large family. The army seemed to offer us a chance for a better life, even though we found ourselves fighting in a strange country for a cause that was not ours.
>
> If at any time you are charged with aiding me in sending information to the British, you may show this letter. I swear that you, Lemuel Hooper, knew nothing of my actions.
>
> Max Hammerstrom

"So that clears Lemuel Hooper's name," Marie said. "Only two hundred years too late."

"But it's not too late to save the house." Judge McGruder looked at Mr. Cline. "Are you willing to deed the place to the Historical Society, if we can get the airport planners to redesign their parking lot?"

Hooper Cline straightened his stooped shoulders into something like the military posture he must have used for most of his life, and when he spoke his voice was firm and deep. "Of course I am. Let's get at it!"

15

Dear Judge McGruder:

We decided to write this letter together, so we'll each just put our name after the part we added.

Thank you for all your help, Judge. If you hadn't talked to those people from the city planning commission, we could never have saved Treason House in time. Mrs. Reuther called Mr. Cline today and told him that the house is officially a "New Glasgow County Historic Landmark."

Now we hope other people will get interested in the house, too, like we did. (Isabelle da Silva)

My brother and his friends finished washing the walls and ceiling of the room where the fire was, like you told them to do. They griped a lot but they did it. (Arnold "Ham" Schmidt)

Next week we have to go back to school, so we won't have much time to help Mr. Cline fix up the house. We did tell the Historical Society people we'd help lead tours on Saturdays when the place is ready. They gave Mr. Cline some money to buy paint and window glass and stuff, and I think he sort of likes making Treason House look good again. (David Keller)

When Mrs. Reuther and Mr. Long were out here the other day they told us Mrs. Frothingham resigned from the Historical Society. She must have been awfully mad about Treason House! Maybe we should be sorry, but Judge, she didn't really care about history. I mean, she's crazy about old dishes and chairs and stuff like that, but she doesn't seem very interested in people. And if history isn't people, what is it? (Marie Bellotti)

For awhile we thought maybe we should quit calling this place Treason House. After all, the letters proved that Lemuel Hooper wasn't a traitor. And you can't exactly call Max Hammerstrom a traitor, either, since he was working for the British all the time and wasn't an American anyway.

We asked Mr. Cline if we shouldn't change the name to "The Hooper House" or something, but he said no. He thinks it's been called Treason House so long that the name belongs to the house, whether it's right or not. All the Hoopers had to put up with it, so why change now? (David)

Mrs. Reuther told us you're going to meet with the committee to decide how the house will be used after it's fixed up. We have some ideas about that. We're hoping that at least part of the time it can be used by kids. You see, the four of us got in trouble here because we didn't know anything about Treason House and so we didn't care about it. It was just an old wreck to us, a place to play. Now it seems sort of like it's ours, somehow, because we know about it and we've worked in it. You don't want to ruin something that's yours. (Isabelle)

The thing is, we don't want Treason House to turn out to be just another dusty old museum. We want it to be used! What do you think about letting schools go there for some of their history classes? They could read Dave's history and see the frescoes and things and really get back to the old days. (Marie)

Do you remember taking history in school, Judge? Usually it's so boring you can hardly stand it. But nobody would fall asleep in a class at Treason House. ("Ham")

Mrs. Reuther has that code of Max Hammerstrom's figured out, and she's thinking of writing a whole book about spies in the Revolutionary War. We told her our idea about having classes at Treason House, and she thought maybe the University might use a place like that too.

My pop told a reporter at the newspaper about the house. He's writing a feature story on it. I gave him the dates and stuff. (David)

There's still a lot of work to be done out there,

Judge. We want to put up a good fence so nobody can get in and mess it up again. Maybe we could figure out a burglar alarm, too. The "Torture Chamber" could be made into a library to keep all the old books and papers and stuff.

I was counting up the other day, and the four of us have worked at least a hundred hours apiece out here, as you first wanted us to do. My total came to 117½ hours. Well, in a way it was fun. I mean, when we knew the house wasn't going to be wrecked we could see the work was worth doing. We're proud of that old house! But at first, you had to make us do it.

So we were thinking, if you find some more kids like us who get in trouble with the law, you might have them come out and work at 4214 Orchard Lane. (Marie)

Your friends,
The Vandals of Treason House